Another Accident?

Somewhere in the house somebody screamed—a thin, wailing shriek of terror. It sounded like a child—it sounded like Bonnie!

Anise rushed back down the hall, around the turn that led to her room and Bonnie's. Miss Enid was standing behind Laura at the dumbwaiter opening, both of them peering down. Bonnie's screams were coming from the shaft.

"She fell!" Laura cried. "She just opened the door and tumbled down the hole!"

"She must have thought that was the door to her room," Miss Enid said shakily, reaching for the pulley rope. "She didn't fall far —the cage was down on first, and she's here on top of it."

Peering in, Anise saw Bonnie eight or nine feet below, beginning to rise as Miss Enid pulled the rope. Bonnie was sobbing as she came to door level and flung her arms around Anise. "Laura pushed me! She pushed me in!"

Mendocino Menace

Ruth MacLeod

AVON
PUBLISHERS OF BARD, CAMELOT, DISCUS, EQUINOX AND FLARE BOOKS

MENDOCINO MENACE is an original publication of Avon Books. This Work has never before appeared in any form.

AVON BOOKS
A division of
The Hearst Corporation
959 Eighth Avenue
New York, New York 10019

First Avon Printing, June, 1973.

AVON TRADEMARK REG. U.S. PAT. OFF. AND
FOREIGN COUNTRIES, REGISTERED TRADEMARK—
MARCA REGISTRADA, HECHO EN CHICAGO, U.S.A.

Printed in the U.S.A.

Mendocino Menace

CHAPTER 1

We should never have come here, Anise thought, hugging her knees and shivering a little in the damp night air as she sat on the cushioned window seat of her bedroom. Yet, had there been any choice? She opened one of the casement windows and peered out, trying to orient herself to the dark landscape outside the big Victorian mansion.

The fog that had obscured their arrival had been swept away by a whistling gale that blew in from the sea. Moonlight whitened a few scudding clouds and limned the feathery crests of the tall pines and firs along the cliff. Beyond the cliff she could hear the boom of the surf as tremendous breakers crashed against the rocks.

At a frightened cry from the next room, she fumbled her way in the dark through the adjoining bath into Bonnie's room. A night lamp cast a dim glow. Bonnie's eyes were closed, the lids still fluttering slightly with her dreams. She must have cried out in her sleep, Anise decided, yearning over the ten-year-old child who still hadn't shed a tear at the loss of her mother nor protested at being sent far away to live with a father she had never known and had been taught to fear.

Anise remembered the day of the funeral, which was brief and sparsely attended. Frail and withdrawn, Sylvia Lockwood

7

had apparently possessed few friends in life, even fewer in death. Anise had listened in wonder to a eulogy that hardly seemed to apply to the gaunt young woman she had nursed during her fatal illness.

Though not a member of the family, she sat in the draped family alcove, her arm around Bonnie. The little girl was quiet and stony faced in the bewilderment of her grief, as if too numb for tears.

"Sylvia mothered her so possessively it gave her no other life," Bonnie's grandmother had said when she and Mr. Dimmick arrived from Phoenix to make the funeral arrangements. They were the only other mourners in the alcove, a thin, elderly couple dressed in somber black. They had tried to make friends with Bonnie, but she clung to Anise.

"It's only natural," Mr. Dimmick said tolerantly. "She's been in your good care for the past six months, and she hasn't seen us since she was two years old. Do you think it advisable for her to attend the funeral?"

Anise had wondered too, but the child had insisted on going.

"Do you know what a funeral is?" Anise asked as she helped Bonnie put on a soft white dress. She had turned away in distaste from the black outfit her grandmother had bought her.

"Of course." Bonnie regarded her gravely, her dark brown eyes shadowed with pain. "Mother told me a funeral is where they plant you under flowers so the person inside—the real you—can go to heaven. She—"

For a moment Anise thought the child would burst into tears—which would have relieved some of the unchildlike tension. But the dark eyes remained dry and unblinking as she swallowed hard and said, "I'll miss her so much! You won't leave me, will you, Miss Weston?"

"Not while you need me," Anise had promised, hoping fervently it was a promise she could keep, though at the time she could see no possible way. Twenty-one years old, with a living to make as well as an obligation to help her parents put younger brothers and sisters through school, she was in no position to undertake the responsibility for an unrelated child. Yet she doubted that the grandparents really wanted Bonnie either, or could give her the care she needed. That left only her estranged father . . . .

A blast of wind rattled the windows and brought a tang of salt air into the room. Anise shivered as she pulled the blankets higher around Bonnie's shoulders. She regarded the child tenderly for another moment, and then crossed the room to close the windows.

What sort of man was Bonnie's father she wondered as she went back to her own room, wrapping an afghan around herself, to sit again at the window. She had given up the idea of sleep until she could quiet the uneasiness that plagued her. This place was so isolated, so far away from everything familiar, and there were strange sounds throughout the house as if it were inhabited by more family than she had been led to expect.

She wished Gregory Lockwood had been here to welcome his little daughter—then wondered if his presence would have assuaged her uneasiness at all. She had seen him only once, very briefly, and nothing that she had learned about him should make her want to meet him again, yet she found that, in a vaguely exciting way, she was looking forward to it, hoping to revise her first disquieting impression.

There had been a heavy rainstorm the evening two months ago when she had answered the doorbell, thinking Sylvia's doctor had arrived. A dark, austere man was standing on the doorstep in the buffeting wind and rain. Behind him a cab was driving away. Anise was always reluctant to let a stranger into the house. Almost every newspaper carried reports of assault, robbery—or both—some in the same neighborhood.

The man said, "I'm Gregory Lockwood. Sylvia sent for me."

Sylvia had said nothing to her, but, whether or not the man was telling the truth, there was such an air of authority about him that Anise found herself automatically unlatching the screen, her heart beating a strange new tempo as he walked into the hall where she could see him better. His dark eyes deep set under exotically slanted eyebrows; his mouth, grimly tense, had a look of unutterable sadness.

"You're the nurse?" he asked, his glance going to the sleeve of her uniform where she wore her nurse's insignia. As he divested himself of his dripping coat, hat, and scarf, laying them on a side chair, his dark inscrutable gaze was on her in a way that made her sharply conscious of her appearance—her slim figure; her medium-blonde hair that always managed to curl

9

into disarray before the day was over; her face that was bare of makeup, with features, she felt, hardly worth the long brooding appraisal he was giving her.

"Which is Sylvia's room?" he asked, and, although he spoke quietly, there was still the air of authority that made her feel obliged to lead the way to Sylvia's door. Before she could ask her patient whether or not she would accept a visitor, Gregory Lockwood was in the room, dismissing her with a curt word of thanks, and closing the door.

Worried about her exclusion in the face of Sylvia's serious illness, Anise had returned to the room she shared with Bonnie, who was already asleep. As Sylvia's divorced husband and Bonnie's father he undoubtedly had a reason for this visit. Had Sylvia actually sent for him? If not, perhaps, when she phoned her parents the other day on learning she hadn't long to live, they had notified him. Sylvia had spoken so bitterly of the man, it was almost inconceivable she would send for him herself.

For a while Anise heard the two voices in Sylvia's room, alternating between an angry cadence and broken murmurs, his tone low and gruff, hers plaintive. During their conversation the doctor rang the doorbell, but Gregory Lockwood left Sylvia's room and admitted him before Anise could get to the door. Anise lingered in the hallway in case the doctor wanted to summon her for the usual consultation. She heard the men talk briefly. Then Gregory Lockwood came out of the room with an expression that could have been anger, frustration, or both. He strode to the entrance hall, grabbed his overcoat, hat, and scarf and went out into the rainy night without putting them on.

"Come in, Miss Weston," the doctor said to her at the bedroom door. "I've given Mrs. Lockwood an injection of tranquilizer. She's quite upset so you had better stay with her until she goes to sleep."

Sylvia's face was pink and puffy from weeping, her eyes wild as she rocked her head from side to side on the pillow, moaning, "I don't believe him! I won't! He lied to me ten years ago—I know he did!"

"It's all right, Mrs. Lockwood," Anise murmured soothingly, wringing a cloth out of cool water to place on the feverish brow of her patient. "He's gone now."

"He wants Bonnie!" she cried, clutching Anise's arm with

10

her fleshless fingers. "He's always wanted Bonnie—but I'll never let him have her! He's wicked—he's cruel! Call my lawyer, right away! I've got to make sure—"

"It's the middle of the night, dear. We'll call your lawyer first thing in the morning."

Gradually the medication took effect and Sylvia fell into a troubled sleep. The next day she insisted on a visit from her lawyer, and consulted him at length after asking Anise to take Bonnie away somewhere—anywhere out of hearing. Anise took her to a playground down the block where she could keep an eye on the lawyer's car and hurry home to her patient as soon as he left.

Sylvia was staring dully at the ceiling, her face more drawn with anguish than ever. After that she was never quite rational. Whether it was worry or simply the rapid progress of the malignancy attacking her, she went into a delirium that gradually subsided into the coma that preceded death.

After Sylvia's funeral Anise received an even more disconcerting impression of Gregory Lockwood from Bonnie's grandparents.

"We must go right back to Phoenix," Mr. Dimmick had said following a consultation with Sylvia's attorney. "We had hoped to take Bonnie with us, even though we're pretty old to start raising another child. But the lawyer says that under the terms of the divorce, Bonnie's father gets full custody on Sylvia's death. The only way we can get custody is by proving he isn't a fit guardian, or isn't providing a suitable home for her. If that's the case, we're anxious to find out, and we'll need your help. You'll be well paid."

"*My* help?" Anise echoed, knowing she would be no match for the stern, brooding, authoritative man who had visited briefly that stormy night.

"That's right!" Mrs. Dimmick's lips were suddenly tight. "We'd better tell you about Gregory. Sylvia divorced him soon after Bonnie was born. While she was still in the hospital, a pregnant woman came to tell her he was the father of her unborn child. Sylvia didn't want to believe it, but, when she got home and talked to some of the neighbors, they told her the woman had been hanging around the house while she was in the hospital having Bonnie. Before she could question Greg about it, she caught them together, the woman in his arms, so she had to believe it then. And when she blew up, Greg was

11

furious because she wouldn't accept him on faith. Either he had no explanation, or was too angry and stubborn to offer one, so Sylvia rushed to Reno for a quick divorce. Greg married the woman the day it was final. Can you blame Sylvia for refusing to let Greg see Bonnie when he tried to claim visiting privileges?"

No wonder Sylvia was bitter, Anise reflected—yet it didn't seem wise, or even right, to turn a child against her father—especially considering the custody he won on her death. When Anise voiced this opinion, Mr. Dimmick said ruefully, "I guess she expected to live until Bonnie came of age. Gregory wouldn't relinquish all claim to her, and I have to admit he supported them both generously."

"That didn't hurt him!" Mrs. Dimmick scoffed. "He's loaded, and his law firm sent the check every month. Now his attorneys have relayed his request that *you* bring Bonnie to him, Miss Weston."

"*Me?*" Anise pressed her fingers to her throat to still a sudden wild pulse. "Where does he live?"

"In California," Mr. Dimmick replied. "Somewhere along the Mendocino coast. Your plane tickets will be delivered to you at the airport here, and you'll change planes in San Francisco for a small place called Lanesville. Gregory will meet you there—probably in the private plane he flies all over the area to look after his lumber interests. The lawyer said today they'll want you to stay for the summer to help Bonnie adjust to her new home. I hope you'll agree—the salary sounds fabulous."

Anise felt her heart lift in relief. She could keep her promise to Bonnie after all, without neglecting her financial obligations to her own family.

"I'll be glad to," she agreed, a little breathless. "The California coast sounds like a wonderful place to spend the summer."

"Not that part of it!" Mr. Dimmick was tense again. "I can't imagine why Gregory lives there. From all I can learn it's stormy all winter, fogbound in summer, with a surf too dangerous for swimming even where there's a beach. His estate is called Mendolair. It's isolated and hard to get to."

Anise felt her enthusiasm ebbing into uneasiness. "Then how—I mean, if it shouldn't be a good place for Bonnie . . . . If it's so isolated, how would we get away?"

"There must be mail or phone service so you can let us

know." He shook his head. "If there were any way to avoid sending Bonnie there . . . but our hands are tied by the custody arrangement. We'll simply have to depend on you."

Anise had promised to do her best, for she had grown to love Bonnie dearly.

So now they were here at Mendolair, and she wasn't at all sure it was a suitable home for Bonnie. For one thing, Gregory Lockwood hadn't kept his word about meeting them at Lanesville.

The whole trip had been hard on Bonnie. By the time they left the jet transport and boarded a smaller plane in San Francisco, the child seemed physically and emotionally exhausted. She sat beside Anise at the rain-drenched window in listless silence, pain shadowing the brown eyes where flecks of gold used to sparkle. The small mouth drooped and her light brown hair, held by a ribbon in Alice-in-Wonderland fashion, hung as straight and smooth as when it was brushed that morning.

I've got to make her laugh and play as a child should, Anise vowed. Bonnie was never a boistrous child, Sylvia had said. Too shy to make friends easily, she had preferred her mother's company to that of her schoolmates.

Maybe Sylvia fostered that, Anise mused, knowing of other divorcées who had overprotected their children in a subconscious effort to compensate for the loss of a husband's love. It would make it still harder for Bonnie to recover from her own loss now, and to adjust to new surroundings.

As the plane approached the landing field, Anise caught a brief glance of a small town huddled among forested hills in the rain. Once they were on the ground she looked about for Mr. Lockwood's private plane, but no other aircraft was in sight. Grasping Bonnie's cold little hand, she tried to protect her from wind and rain as they sprinted to the small room under the control tower. Wiping rain from her eyes, she searched the room for Bonnie's father, but, aside from two young men behind the counter, there was only one person in the room—a tall, rough-looking, dour-faced man wearing heavy boots, corduroy trousers, a dull plaid mackinaw, and a floppy rain hat. His light gray eyes surveyed them from under beetling brows. Suddenly uneasy, Anise held Bonnie's hand tighter and hurried over to the counter.

13

"I'm expecting Mr. Lockwood," she began, but by then the man was beside her, touching the sleeve of her tweed coat.

"Mr. Lockwood sent me. I'm to drive you to Mendolair. He's tied up at the mill and couldn't come."

Anise stared at him doubtfully, not liking the hawk-nosed, hard-faced look of the man, but the clerk behind the counter spoke up. "It's all right, ma'am. This is Mr. Morton—George Morton. He's caretaker over at Mendolair. I'll get your baggage for him."

Mr. Morton had come in a truck. "We need four-wheel drive after we leave the pavement," he explained. He spread a tarpaulin over their baggage in the bed of the truck, and helped them climb into the cab, Bonnie in the middle. The narrow, two-lane highway wound through tall forests, so darkened by rain and clouds that Mr. Morton had the headlights on bright. There was almost no oncoming traffic and Anise began to feel as if they were following a long tortuous tunnel into nowhere.

"I'm scared," Bonnie whimpered, snuggling close as they braced themselves against the swinging curves.

"Could we go a little slower?" Anise asked meekly. "I'm afraid Bonnie might get carsick."

The man gave Bonnie a glance of annoyance, and if he reduced speed at all it was barely perceptible. "I hope she's not a sickly child. Mendolair's no health resort, and there's no doctor at your beck and call if she starts ailing."

"She's not sickly! But the way you take these curves—"

"Okay, okay, I'll slow down, but I gotta get back to my work. I was up to my ears in a job when Mr. Gregory phoned and said I'd have to hustle over here and pick you up."

"How far is it?" Anise asked, holding Bonnie close as they rounded another fast curve.

"About eighty-five miles, but it'll seem like hundreds poking along like this. Rain slows us up enough without . . . ."

He let the sentence dangle and for over an hour they followed the winding highway through dense forest, climbing steeply, descending the sharp curves only to cross a ravine and climb again. Gradually the rain subsided and an occasional bar of yellow sunlight slanted through the woods, sparkling on the dripping branches of cedar, fir, and pine. Now and then a wild burst of color flowered near the highway—all shades of rose and lavender. Mr. Morton said it was rhododendron. Finally they rounded a steep crag and came out above the blue sunlit ocean.

"How beautiful!" Anise cried, hearing Bonnie's slight gasp beside her. From this point they could see for miles up the jagged coastline and watch the blue water crashing against the rocks or foaming onto a sandy crescent of a beach in some cove.

"Are we almost there?" Bonnie asked, quinting against the brightness.

Mr. Morton made a sound of derision. "Hardly got a good start."

The highway left the cliffs to angle back through the forests, or past meadows where cattle grazed. The next time they could see the ocean, there was a dull gray strip along the horizon.

"Fog's startin' to roll in," Mr. Morton grumbled.

The dark layer thickened and rose. It soon obliterated the sun and turned the bright blue of the ocean to a dull green before the highway left the coast to wind through woods and meadows again. Eventually the fog penetrated the forest, and, when the road once again came out on a cliff above the sea, darkness had deepened the mist and the ocean was no longer visible.

For the rest of the trip, the fog was so dense that the beam of the headlights seemed to be shining on an opaque wall. Anise wondered how Mr. Morton could follow the winding road, but he seemed to know the way by instinct. After miles of this he turned off the pavement onto a boulder-rough roadbed that nearly jolted them out of the seat. Bonnie, who had fallen asleep with her head in Anise's lap, sat up with a cry of alarm.

"Just hang on tight," Mr. Morton said gruffly. He had proved to be a taciturn traveling companion, concentrating on his driving, answering her questions so grudgingly that she gave up trying to talk. Her spirits sank as she wondered with deep foreboding what sort of place Bonnie's new home would be—and how they would escape should it prove necessary.

"Why doesn't Mr. Lockwood make the county smooth this road out?" she complained, clinging to Bonnie so the child wouldn't fall off the seat.

"'Tain't county property. It's his own private road and he don't want it good enough to attract tourists here to ruin our beaches. It's used mostly for delivery trucks. He takes the

15

plane himself. Those of us who don't fly just put up with the bumps."

"Who else lives on the estate?" Anise was anxious to learn more now that the man finally seemed willing to talk.

"His an' his wife's family, mostly. We try to keep the place livable, but it's pretty rugged, an' I feel like I should warn you the best thing you could do for this little girl is get her away from Mendolair as soon as you can."

"Why?" she demanded, her uneasiness mounting.

He was scowling at the road as he eased the truck over a bed of boulders, and for a while she thought he wasn't going to answer. Then he growled in an undertone, "It just ain't gonna be healthy for her, that's all I got to say." Gathering speed again, he swerved around a crag, over a rustic bridge onto a wide level space, and drove toward an immense house which could be seen dimly through the fog. There he stopped the truck with a jolt and switched off the motor and headlights, saying, "Okay, climb out—this here's Mendolair."

CHAPTER 2

Anise rose from the window seat, finding her joints stiff from tension and the chill damp air. She started to close the casement window, then on an impulse opened it wider and peered down through the darkness below, wondering if these rooms were above the front door where Mr. Morton had let them out of the truck. In the misty darkness it had been hard to see.

A wild, unearthly yowl below the window brought her to startled attention. It was followed by a scratching sound, coming closer and closer, then another yowl, almost at window level, but closer to Bonnie's windows than to these. Anise tried to still the rocking of her heart as she leaned out farther, peering through the gloom. There was a thumping of approaching feet now, like some sort of creature running, then more sounds of scratching, and a rustling through leaves accompanied by heavy panting. She stood trembling for a long moment, realizing that a person could probably climb to these windows. When the porch lamp had been switched on at their arrival, she had observed a lighted portion of the frame building with a great deal of old-fashioned gingerbread ornamentation. A fretwork balustrade enclosed the narrow porch and was repeated around a small balcony above a heavy oak door. From

17

seeing these details, Anise imagined the rest of the house as being composed of many wings, turrets, and cupolas. There should be plenty of footholds for anyone to climb—and she could find no locks on these windows.

A dog barked and she relaxed with a shamed chuckle. This place must really be bothering me, she thought, if a dog can make my heart pound so hard. The scratching and yowling was probably a cat, being chased by the dog.

She turned away from the window, then swung back in sharp new concern at the sound of footsteps running toward the house—no animal this time, but a heavily shod person.

"Mancho! Mancho!" someone called in a husky, breathless tone. It wasn't Mr. Morton. It hardly sounded like a man's voice, yet it was not a woman's either. It might be an adolescent boy whose voice was in the process of changing. His words were indistinct and gutteral as he went on, "Mancho! Bad boy! You leave Leo be!" His next words were lost in a rough scrambling sound, as if boy and dog were rolling around together.

Who could it be? Anise wondered. Some member of Gregory's family? Or his wife's family? Was Gregory still married to the woman Sylvia's parents had told her about?

As the boy and dog moved away from the house she leaned out the window again, glanced in the direction of Bonnie's room, and saw a pair of green lights that frightened her until she realized they were a cat's eyes. It was in a tree where she couldn't remember a tree, so these windows must not face the front after all.

She went to bed shivering and wondered if she could ever sleep in this place. She had been on edge ever since the heavy front door slowly opened at their arrival, and a gaunt woman came out, almost as tall as Mr. Morton. Her graying hair was skinned back into a bun. Her striped dress was tight at the waist with a full skirt much longer than the current style, a crisp white apron tied over it.

"My wife, she's the housekeeper," Mr. Morton had said, nodding toward the woman as he pulled baggage out from under the tarpaulin.

"So you're Bonnie," Mrs. Morton murmured, gazing at the child so intensely that Bonnie shrank against Anise with a shiver. Just then a huge tawny cat lunged from the dim interior behind the woman, stopping at sight of them to arch its

18

back, enlarge its waving tail, and show a small pink tongue as it spat at them. The woman bent to swoop the animal up in her arms, not taking her eyes from Bonnie.

"Shut up, Leo," she said absently, scratching its head, and the cat subsided, beginning to purr against her shoulder. Mrs. Morton finally took her gaze from Bonnie and turned to Anise. "You're that nurse? I hope you're a good one if the kid gets sick. There's nobody around here. I tried to tell Mr. Gregory it's no place for her, but he's stubborn as they come. By the time he finds out I'm right, it'll be too late. Well, come on in. Mr. Greg ain't back yet, but I'm supposed to make you welcome."

Anise felt anything but welcome as she followed the woman's stiff back into the dim hallway. Bonnie tugged at her hand, stretched upward to whisper loudly, "Do we have to stay here? I'm scared!"

"It's all right, honey," Anise murmured, hoping she sounded more assured than she felt. "We can't leave now, but maybe everything will seem better tomorrow."

At the top of the stairway an overhead light shone down a narrow hall, both sides punctuated by closed doors. After turning into another hall she opened a door and ushered them into a large room that was flooded with light from a sparkling chandelier whose prisms sent rainbows dancing across the walls.

Anise caught a sharp breath and felt Bonnie's hand relax slightly in hers. The room was lovely. Its floors were thickly carpeted, its walls bright with excellent paintings, mostly scenic views of mountains or a rugged coastline. An inviting four-poster bed occupied one corner. A number of comfortable-looking chairs were scattered about among an assortment of small tables. At one side there was a Sheraton desk and a bookcase filled with books still in their bright dust jackets.

Mrs. Morton put the cat down and moved to the small hearth between heavily draped windows. She lighted a match to the crumpled paper under a symmetrical stack of kindling and logs.

"You need a fire to cut the dampness this close to the ocean," she said as flames leaped up to crackle through the kindling. "Our only other heat is a butane furnace and I'm scared of that explosive stuff—'specially with that tank out on the porch. Couldn't dig into the rocks to put it underground,

19

but every time the truck comes to fill it . . . . Well, we have to cook our food and heat the house somehow."

She turned from the fire to give Bonnie further inspection in the brighter light. "So you're Bonnie," she repeated with a worried expression. "Your daddy has a room ready for you too. Come this way."

Bonnie clung to Anise's hand as they followed the woman to a door at one side, through a roomy bathroom with a long clawfoot tub, into another bedroom, obviously a child's room, done in blue and white. There was a lace canopy over the bed, and a small crystal chandelier. The carpet was thick white pile, and two of the pale blue walls were lined with white painted shelves, each loaded with toys and books. A fire was laid on a small hearth in here also, and Mrs. Morton touched a match to it, then showed Anise the cupboard where more wood was stacked.

"George will bring your things up," she added, "and I'll serve dinner in your room, Miss Weston. Anything else you want?"

Anise shook her head and the woman left. In the other room they found the cat curled up before the fire. Bonnie went over to sit cautiously beside it. "Do you think he'll bite if I pet him?" she asked.

Anise wasn't sure. The cat had looked vicious when it first lunged from the house to spit at them. She knelt to stroke its back lightly. The cat stretched and began to purr. Then Bonnie petted him too, her little face lighting with more pleasure than she had shown since her mother's death. She had always loved animals, Sylvia had once said, but had never had a pet of her own.

"Mrs. Morton called him Leo," Bonnie said, scratching its head. She frowned and looked up thoughtfully. "I don't think I like Mrs. Morton. She looks at me sort of funny."

"I know, honey, but she's only the housekeeper. When your daddy comes home maybe we'll feel more comfortable. He must be very thoughtful to have such lovely rooms ready for us here."

Even as she spoke, a vision of Gregory Lockwood returned to her mind, the way he had looked that stormy night, austere, brooding, as if struggling with some inner problem. Of course there was nothing pleasant about visiting a dying exwife years after a bitter parting. He must have been planning Bonnie's arrival ever since. Anise wished again that he could have been here tonight to give Bonnie a warm welcome.

Suddenly the air was rent by a screeching sound somewhere in the hallway, followed by a loud clattering and a series of bumps. Anise caught Bonnie in her arms as they both sprang to their feet. They were staring at the door when it opened and Mrs. Morton came through, pushing a cart on which the sound of rattling dishes could be heard from under a white damask cloth.

"My stars, you look scared stiff!" the woman exclaimed, appearing surprised. Then she chuckled. "I know—it was that old dumb waiter screechin' that scared you! The pulleys or something need oil an' I keep telling George he oughta fix it."

Mr. Morton came behind her, loaded with their baggage which he deposited beside a closet, then went after more while Mrs. Morton spread the damask cloth on a small table and served their dinner.

"George caught the fish in the surf," she said, "an' we raised the peas and potatoes. Everything else, Mr. Greg usually brings in the plane. He needs to stock up the freezer again, or else George will have to jog down to the general store at the cape. Ain't much choice there, though."

"Why does Mr. Lockwood live in such an out-of-the-way place?" Anise asked, since the woman seemed more friendly now. Expecting a casual answer, such as that he liked the climate or the scenery, or it was near his lumber interests, Anise was dismayed to see the woman's face grow cold and remote, the gaunt angles bitter.

"He has his reasons—whether we agree with him or not," she said. She picked up the sleeping cat from the hearth and went to the door, pausing to say, "Pile your dishes on the cart and shove it out in the hall when you're through. Good night."

"I don't like her," Bonnie said, staring at the closed door.

Anise couldn't say she did either, but to the child she murmured, "I guess she means well. She seems unhappy about something. We may like her when we know her better."

"I don't like Mr. Morton either," Bonnie went on gravely. "I don't like this whole place! I want to go home!"

"This is your home now, dear. I'm sure it will seem better tomorrow."

Thinking back to those assuring words now as she tossed and turned in her bed, trying to sleep, Anise wondered if they would ever feel comfortable here. The wind was dying now, and the intermittent bawling of a foghorn somewhere in the distance told her the fog must have rolled back in. When she finally managed to doze off, the unearthly screech of the dumb waiter woke her up again. There were other strange noises throughout the house, and finally a light touch on her face brought her upright, her heart pounding as she gasped, "What's that?"

"It's me," Bonnie said in a quavery voice. "I'm scared. Can I get in bed with you?"

"Of course! Then maybe we can both sleep."

Bonnie was trembling, but she gradually quieted, cuddling close, and apparently went to sleep. Anise wished she could spirit her away to some pleasant place where the wounds of her early childhood could heal. How long would it take—and how much would they have to endure—before the court would judge this an unsuitable home for her? Or would things seem much better after Gregory Lockwood returned to take charge?

Anise was more wakeful than ever now, for the whole house seemed awake. She heard footsteps sounding here and there, sometimes running hard. Once she was sure she heard somebody sobbing.

When finally she slept she was plagued by nightmares that periodically woke her. At daylight she awoke with a start when her door was thrust open and the cart rolled in, clattering with dishes. She sat up and stared at the woman pushing it —a much younger person than Mrs. Morton, wearing the white cap and apron of a maid.

"You folks still asleep?" she asked cheerfully, switching on the light. "Mom sent your breakfast. You better get up and eat while it's hot. I'm Deirdre Morton."

Bonnie was sitting up now, rubbing her eyes, looking as sleepy and confused as Anise felt.

"I'll light a fire," Deirdre said in the same cheerful voice, "while you get washed and put on a robe or something. Might as well not bother to dress yet. You won't want to go anywhere this morning. The fog's like pea soup outside."

Washed, combed, and robed, they returned to the room to find a crackling fire warming the air and the draperies pulled back from windows that were a misty blank from the fog. Deirdre was placing plates of bacon, eggs, and toast on the little table. The fragrance of hot fresh coffee was tantalizing.

"There's milk for the little one," Deirdre said. "It may taste different at first because it's been frozen. But she'll get used to it."

With her eyes focusing better now, Anise saw that the girl slightly resembled her mother, but was more cheerful and relaxed. Her brown hair was cut short, her cheeks were pink and round, her blue eyes bright with curiosity as she gazed at Bonnie.

"She don't take after Mr. Greg much, does she? I'm surprised he'd want to bring her here—but I guess he didn't know what else to do with her."

"Why wouldn't he want to bring her here?" Anise asked quickly, hoping Deirdre would explain her parents' rather resentful attitude, and the vague menace that seemed to envelop the place. But the girl's face promptly became tight with caution.

"I shouldn't have said that. It's just that she comes from a different side of the family and—well, I wondered how the others. . . . Then it's so lonesome and far away from everything. But Mr. Greg bought her a lot of books and toys. You both better stay in today. With fog so thick you could get lost the minute you step outside. I'll come back for your dishes in a little while." She left.

"I don't want to stay shut up in here all day," Bonnie said. "Couldn't we look around and see what made all the scary noises last night?"

"I think so, honey." Anise would like to see the rest of the house too, and meet the other members of the family. Her uneasiness during the long night had abated with daylight—but she hoped the fog would soon give way to sunshine.

They had eaten and dressed by the time Deirdre returned to make their beds and remove the chart of dishes. Accustomed to doing her own work, Anise helped with the bedmaking, in spite of Deirdre's protests.

"We'd like to go downstairs and meet the family," Anise said as the maid was leaving. "Shall we find our own way?"

Deirdre paused with her hand on the doorknob. "I—I don't know . . . . Of course it's all right for you to go downstairs, but the family . . . I mean, I don't think Mrs. Lockwood will be leaving her own room today, or wanting any visitors—she hasn't been very well. You may have heard us rushing around in the night taking care of her?"

23

So that's what the commotion had been about, Anise reflected. The sobbing too?

"This afternoon," Deirdre went on, "Laura will come out to play, but she has to have her lessons in the morning."

"Laura?" Anise asked quickly.

"The Lockwoods' little girl. She has a suite with her governess in another part of the house. Why don't you wait here until Mom has time to show you around the place? It's pretty big." She wheeled the cart of dishes out and closed the door.

I suppose we could amuse ourselves here all day if necessary, Anise thought as she looked over the vast supply of games and toys in Bonnie's room. They chose a new game to play and were engrossed in it half an hour later when Mrs. Morton came in, dressed exactly as when she had met them last night, her face still gaunt and unfriendly.

"Deirdre says you'd like to look around the house," she said with a faint smile. "I'll show you the main rooms but we better not go to Mrs. Lockwood's wing until she's feeling better. Maybe after lunch you can walk down to the beach. Fog's beginning to thin out a little. But don't wander off an' get lost."

She led them along the dim hall, down the carpeted stairs to the entrance Anise remembered from last night. Sliding oak doors opened into a huge room, obviously the living room. It was beautifully furnished in a Victorian style to match the exterior of the building, but it looked as if it were seldom used. The grand piano in one corner was closed and covered with a vari-colored, fringed silk scarf. The thick carpeting was faded below the windows where the draperies were pulled back. Some of the chairs were of carved teakwood, probably more decorative than comfortable, but there were a few pieces of upholstered furniture that looked inviting. A small fire seemed lost, burning weakly in an immense fireplace.

"The library's on through here," Mrs. Morton said, leading them through portiéres made of strung eucalyptus pods. The alcove was about half the size of the living room. A massive desk and straight-backed chairs occupied the center, and the walls were lined with books. "These are all old books—Mr. Greg put the new ones in your suite. The eating rooms are across the hall—this way."

The formal dining room was large and stately and like the living room looked as if it were seldom used. The breakfast room, beyond it, was bright and cheerful. A round maple table was surrounded by captain's chairs under a bright brass chandelier. A window seat across one side was covered with gay cretonne cushions matching the curtains that were drawn back from the wide expanse of windows. The fog was now thinning enough so that the ghostly shape of trees showed through the mist.

"I don't think there's anyplace else you'd care to see right away," Mrs. Morton said, "Except for the kitchen and pantry, the rest is mostly bedrooms and suites like yours. Look around if you like, but I got work to do now."

Anise glanced down at Bonnie and saw the small shoulders shrug. "I like it better up in our rooms," Bonnie said. "Let's go back and finish our game."

CHAPTER 3

At noon a gong sounded and Deirdre opened Bonnie's door to inform them the bell meant that lunch would be served in the breakfast room in ten minutes. Anise hoped other members of the household would be present, but the table was set for only two, and Deirdre was there to serve them.

"Doesn't anyone else eat here?" Anise asked.

Deirdre shook her head "Not for lunch today. Laura's with her mother, and Mr. Gregory isn't back yet."

The sun came out while they were eating, and from the row of windows they could see a tree-shaded garden in full bloom, spreading to the cliff where a tall pine was etched against a blue sky.

"It must be pleasant down on the beach now," Anise said when Deirdre returned to ask if they wanted more dessert. "It's all right if we go down for a while, isn't it?"

The girl nodded. "Take the path through the garden. It leads to the top of the stairs down the cliff. But don't go climbing over the rocks down on the beach—stay in the cove."

The garden was bright with flowers, and cascades of red, coral, and purple fuschias bloomed on bushes or hung from baskets. Roses of every hue bloomed profusely along with aza-

26

leas, and huge clumps of rhododendron like those they had seen in the woods on the way to Mendolair yesterday.

A rickety-looking stairway led down the precipitous cliff, but it felt steady enough underfoot as they gingerly made their way down. The sandy beach below lay in a white arc. A mild blue portion of the sea lazily foamed to the shore, its waves small and sedate compared to those crashing against the rocky point at each end of the cove. Reaching the beach, Bonnie excitedly pulled off her shoes and socks to run down to the wet sand and wait for a wave to swish up over her feet. Impulsively, Anise joined the child in the shallow, tingling-cold surf.

Bonnie was fascinated as they wandered along the beach, and Anise also found it exciting. The sand sparkled with glittering rock chips, some she suspected were semiprecious stones, for she was sure she recognized agate, jade, and jasper. There were also curiously formed pieces of driftwood, attractive seashells in pastel shades, and mussels, sand dollars, and starfish. In the tide pools there were live sea creatures she couldn't identify, but she watched them with as much interest as Bonnie whose wide brown eyes were now flecked with gold again at each new discovery.

As the tide went farther out they could climb the barnacle-encrusted rocks enclosing the cove and see up and down the jagged shoreline. Steep craggy inlets and rugged promontories plunged into the surf. Remembering Deirdre's warning, they returned to the little beach.

Finally tiring of chasing waves and examining rocks, shells, and sea creatures, they lay on the warm sand nearer the cliff to let the sun dry their splashed skirts.

"We should have brought a towel," Anise said, trying to wipe sand from Bonnie's damp feet. The sea was getting rougher now as the tide turned. Waves crashed harder and closer in against the rocks at each end of the protected cove. Swimming now appeared so dangerous that she was surprised to see two dark figures emerge from the water at one of the rocky points, dive from a ledge and swim strongly toward shore. When they stood up in the shallow surf she saw that they were wearing black neoprene suits, with scuba diving equipment on their backs. Both headed toward the stairway but one of them, on catching sight of Anise and Bonnie, turned sharply to come over and confront them.

"This is a private beach," he began gruffly, then his jaw

27

dropped and his eyes widened to give Bonnie closer inspection. "I bet you're Greg's other kid, aren't you! He said you'd be coming here—but I didn't know it would be so soon."

He was sturdy and broad-shouldered, but otherwise, even though he had removed his face mask, it was hard to judge his appearance with his helmet on.

"Yes, this is Bonnie," Anise told him spiritedly. "Who are you?"

He grinned and turned his attention to her. "I'm Greg's brother-in-law, Bart Graham, and I suppose you're the kid's nurse? Well, let me welcome you both to Mendolair—but I bet you don't stay long unless you're pretty thick-skinned. Some of the family aren't too happy about another heir making an appearance. They thought Sylvia's share had been settled on her long ago."

His smile was tight as he shrugged and turned to walk over to the stairs. The other diver had climbed to the top and was disappearing over the cliff. Bart was about halfway up when a little girl about Bonnie's age came running down the zigzag stairs, her long blonde hair flying. She grabbed Bart's hand and danced beside him up the rest of the steps, talking excitedly, but a rising wind picked up her voice and Anise couldn't hear the words.

So that's Laura, Gregory's daughter by that other woman, Anise reflected somberly. Apparently the family had expected his fortune to come to her! Was Bonnie in danger, considered a threat to that inheritance?

Shivering as the wind turned colder, Anise hurriedly helped Bonnie with her shoes and socks, donned her own, and they started up the stairs. Breathless at the top, they paused and saw Bart standing with Laura on the porch.

"Shall we go in and get acquainted with your—your half sister?" Anise asked Bonnie, but the child's innate shyness held her back.

"I don't like that man. Let's take a walk first." She tugged Anise's hand in the opposite direction.

"Okay, but we mustn't go far," Anise agreed uneasily. Up here the wind wasn't as cold, especially after they passed a row of sheltering trees and following a path that led into a wooded area.

Though she had been warned about getting lost, it seemed safe enough here where the path was plain, wide, and looked well traveled. They could turn back as soon as they felt they had walked far enough.

It was quiet in the forest as the path narrowed and began to wind in an intriguing way that made it exciting to see what was around each next turn. Anise recognized some of the trees as spruce, pine, fir, and red alder, forming a canopy overhead. There was lush undergrowth of ferns and moss, here and there patches of huckleberry, salal, azalea, and rhododendron. At one point they found a tall stand of redwood, the columns gleaming bright among the other trees. It was here they became aware of a loud squawking that approached from somewhere in the woods. Anise felt Bonnie's small hand clutch hers and tremble as the squawks came closer.

"Bluejays!" Anise cried as she saw the flash of wings among the trees. There must be fifty of them, she thought. They formed a noisy flock, staying together as they flew from tree to tree, following a definite course through the woods.

"They're stellar's jays," Anise said, remembering that she had read about the big, dark blue, crested birds.

Suddenly a cat appeared from the underbrush to slink swiftly up the path ahead. As if at a signal, all the jays swooped down in dive-bombing precision, making passes at the cat until it hid again in the underbrush.

"It's Leo!" Bonnie cried, running to the spot where the cat had disappeared. "Make the birds leave him alone!" She picked up a small fallen branch and waved it frantically toward the birds, crying, "Shoo! Shoo!"

As if he knew he had a protector now, the cat came out of the underbrush and ran along the path, Bonnie following and waving her branch, shouting at the frustrated birds that continued to hover and squawk, but no longer made such close passes.

Laughing, Anise followed along too, glad that Bonnie had found something to take her mind off her grief over her mother and her initial dislike of this place. Maybe it would be good for her here after all—if only there were no danger from some member of the family who resented her arrival. Would it be Laura? Surely the child was too young to care about an inheritance. Who, then? Laura's mother? Or was it Bart, resenting Bonnie on Laura's behalf? He and the child had certainly looked companionable climbing the stairs. He would be her

29

uncle—her mother's brother. Had he hoped to scare Bonnie away?

Or were there others involved whom she hadn't met yet? What about the husky-voiced boy with a dog named Mancho? Who was the other diver with Bart? The Dimmicks had apparently known little about the Lockwoods except for Gregory—and they didn't trust him.

When the cat was finally lost to sight, and the jays had squawked off in the distance, Anise decided it was time to turn back. The forest was growing darker and, looking up, she saw wisps of fog drifting in among the crests of the taller trees.

They hadn't retraced their steps far before the path divided, both arms of the Y looking exactly alike. "Which way did we come?" Anise asked Bonnie, but the child couldn't remember either. They studied the ground carefully, looking for signs of their coming, but there were no footprints on the thick layer of pine needles. They must have passed this point while following the cat, she thought—that's why they hadn't noticed. She chose the fork that seemed to lead toward the sea, but after following its intricate curves for a while, making choices at other places where it divided, she found such a maze of crisscross trails that she had no idea where they were, or in which direction the house lay. Now more fog was rolling in, dripping from the trees, darkening the forest.

"I'm scared," Bonnie whimpered, "and I'm tired."

"I'm tired too," Anise admitted, "but we must keep on walking until we find our way back."

She tried calling, yelling at the top of her lungs, but her voice only reverberated through the trees, coming back to them in a hollow echo as if it had bounced against some cliff. Bonnie walked doggedly along beside her, looking ready to cry, and Anise felt tears of frustration sting her own eyes.

Gradually the trees and underbrush thinned out and a final turn brought them to the edge of a small clearing. At first Anise thought they had reached the house, then she saw that it was only a small cottage. But maybe someone there could take them home—or at least direct the way.

As they started forward again, a huge spotted dog bounded from the open doorway, barking and snarling viciously, showing its long sharp teeth. Anise cringed back, flinging a protective arm around Bonnie to hold her close. About thirty feet from the door the dog stopped with a jerk that brought him up

30

on his hind legs, pawing the air, still snarling and baring his teeth, lolling tongue slavering as he struggled to get loose.

Anise saw then that he was leashed to a chain that was tethered to something inside the house. With a sigh of relief she patted Bonnie's shoulder. "It's all right, honey—he's tied up so he can't get to us."

A shadow moved across the window and Anise called out, hoping now for help. Instead of answering, however, whoever was inside apparently untethered the dog, for again he bounded toward them with his ferocious barking and snarling, dragging his chain.

Picking Bonnie up bodily, Anise turned to run, though she knew she couldn't possibly outdistance the big dog, even if her terror hadn't made every limb weak and shaky and her feet so numb they dragged. It was like a nightmare—Bonnie too much of a load, the path rough, the dog's snarls coming closer. A root caught her foot and she went sprawling on top of Bonnie, trembling and helpless. She tried to protect the child's body with her own as she waited in horror for the snarling beast to attack.

"Mancho! Stop! Stay!" It was the voice she had heard below her window last night, clipping the words in the same husky tone. The snarling stopped, and there was silence except for the sound of the dog's heavy panting, and the thrashing of footsteps through underbrush nearby.

Anise sat up, still holding Bonnie close as they looked back. The young man who rushed up to grab the dog's collar could be in his teens or twenties. She recognized the mongoloid type —the small head on a large body, the sparse hair and folded eyelids, the flat-rooted nose above a short upper lip. Whatever his chronological age, his mental age was probably between four and seven.

"He won't hurt you now," the boy said thickly. "His name is Mancho 'cause he's spotted. He won't bite when I tell him not to." He added something else too indistinct for her to understand.

"Thank you so much!" she said fervently, helping Bonnie to her feet. She wondered if this boy would tell them how to get home—or if he even knew. She could hardly hope for help from anyone inside the cottage, since someone in there had let the dog loose.

While she was searching for simple words to ask for directions, she heard a small plane overhead. The boy looked up and said something that sounded like "Mr. Lockwood."

So Bonnie's father was returning at last—in spite of the fog, which didn't seem as dense in the clearing as in the dimness of the forest. She could see the plane circling high above, looking ghostly in the thin mist.

"Where does he land?" she asked. "Is there an airstrip somewhere around here? Could we get there right away?"

The boy pointed to a trail that led uphill and around a sharp crag just above the cottage. Anise thanked him and tried to hurry Bonnie, who was exhausted now. If they could reach the airstrip in time to catch Mr. Lockwood before he left it, he would show them the way back to the house.

It was farther to the crag than it had looked, and when the trail became steep, Bonnie was almost too tired to struggle on.

"Soon we'll be at the top, then it will be easy to go down," Anise comforted, urging her on. Her own legs were shaking with fatigue and she vowed with every step that she would never again take Bonnie through the woods, no matter how safe and fascinating the path might look!

As they approached the crag they found themselves above the fog. A sudden scampering nearby made them stop and grab each other in new fear.

"Look!" Bonnie gasped, and Anise breathed a sigh of relief as a small furry creature with a big fluffy tail went leaping over a bed of rocks and slate.

"It's a squirrel, honey—it won't hurt us." The squirrel changed direction, made a circle, then sat up on its haunches to sniff the air before starting to run in a zigzag pattern. Anise suddenly realized that the animal was terrified, and the next moment she saw why. A shadow passed over it, then a huge bird swooped down to grab it in sharp talons and fly away.

Bonnie screamed, and Anise caught her close. "That was an eagle, honey. It—" She broke off as a blast of gunfire thundered from a wooded area just below. Someone shot at the bird and its prey, she thought, but had missed completely, for the eagle was still spiraling off into the misty distance, the squirrel in its talons.

Holding Bonnie's hand, she started climbing again. Suddenly her heart jolted with new terror as another shot blasted from the woods, chipping hunks of earth and rock from the crag right above them.

"He's shooting at *us!*" she cried, ducking low as she caught Bonnie close. She glanced back down the trail, saw that they would be targets all the way if they tried to return. Besides, whoever was shooting was located in that direction. Thrusting Bonnie ahead to shield her, holding her low, she scrambled on up the trial which seemed to disappear around the crag. With every step she expected to feel a bullet pierce her back, but though another blast sounded, she managed to push Bonnie over the hump, around to the other side of the crag where they were out of range.

For a long moment she stood holding Bonnie close, panting and trembling. "Thank the Lord he was a poor shot," she gasped, then taking Bonnie's hand again she added urgently, "Let's get away from here!"

Skidding in the loose rock and shale, slipping and sliding, she tried to study the panorama spread out before them, the ocean almost lost in fog beyond the forest to their left, and off to the right a flat cleared surface which must be the airstrip. That was confirmed when the plane circled once more and came in for a landing. It taxied to a stop and a man got out, shutting off the noisy motor. Anise cupped her hands about her mouth like a megaphone and yelled as loud as she could. The man halted in his walk across the field, and looked up.

"How do we get down?" Anise called, separating the words to pronounce each one distinctly. He pointed to her right where a faint trail could be seen. Calling again, asking him to wait, she led Bonnie down the trail into a scrubby woods. When they came into the clear again, the man was hiking up the trial toward them. He must be Mr. Lockwood, though he hardly looked at all as she remembered him. Probably because he wore different clothes, she decided, slacks and sweater over a sports shirt open at the throat. Nor did his hair and eyebrows seem dark out here as they had indoors at night.

"What the hell were you doing up there on the crag?" he demanded as soon as they were within hearing distance. "Don't you know you might—" He stopped short and stared, looking as blank as Anise suddenly felt.

"You're not Mr. Lockwood!" she cried, for she could see now that he definitely was not the man who had visited Sylvia.

"Yes, I'm Clay—Greg's brother," he replied, his fascinated

33

gaze on Bonnie. So there were two Mr. Lockwoods, Anise reflected, which accounted for the Mortons calling Bonnie's father Mr. Gregory.

"I'm sorry," Clay said, glancing at Anise. "I thought Enid had taken Laura out of bounds again. I'd forgotten you were arriving today—or was it yesterday?" He held out his hand to Bonnie, frowning as she cringed and clung to Anise.

"Don't be afraid of me, honey. I'm your uncle. We're going to be great friends. Your daddy is busy at the mill so he asked me to take care of you and help you feel at home." He smiled, and gradually the child relaxed, laying her hand in the palm he held out to her.

He turned to Anise. "You're Miss Weston. Greg says Sylvia thought the world of you. Welcome to Mendolair! You were very kind to bring Bonnie to us here."

Anise let her hand be cupped in his, breathing easy at last. This was the first warm welcome they had received and her heart went out to the pleasant young man. He wasn't quite as tall as his brother, and his features were milder—full lips, an almost snub nose, light brown hair and eyebrows. The brows didn't have that winglike slant either, yet his eyes were deep set and hooded like Gregory's.

He release her hand and bent to take Bonnie in his arms. "I'll show you the easiest way down to the hangar where I parked the jeep. After I put the airplane away, check it over and refuel for the next trip, I'll drive you home."

CHAPTER 4

The hangar seemed to be embedded in the foot of the cliff. Anise and Bonnie waited in the jeep while Clay serviced the small plane and stowed it away. By the time he joined them, more fog could be seen rolling in, obscuring the sky.

"What on earth were you doing up at the crag?" Clay asked as he started the motor. "Didn't anyone tell you it's dangerous to wander far from the house before you know your way around? You could really be lost after the fog rolls in."

"You can be sure we won't go near that crag again!" Anise retorted. "Somebody shot at us up there! Probably the same person who turned that vicious dog loose on us!"

"No!" He glanced at her sharply. "You must be mistaken! Mancho breaks loose now and then—he's getting so big and strong. I'll warn George about that. As for the shots, someone must have been hunting. There's plenty of game around— deer, marmots, squirrels, birds—and poachers aren't always particular about seasons. Did you see or hear any sort of creature around that—"

"Only an eagle that caught a squirrel—and the shots didn't follow its flight. They spattered on the cliff right above *us*!"

"I'm terribly sorry," he said, sounding sincere. "I'll caution the household—but I doubt it was anyone from Mendolair.

Probably tourists from the State Park up the coast. I'm sure it was accidental, you were mistaken for a cougar or something. Why would anyone shoot at you and Bonnie?"

"I don't know." She was still unconvinced. "A skin diver who called himself Bart Graham told us Bonnie might be resented as an unwelcome heir."

"Hogwash! Bart suffers from an overactive imagination and reads too many murder mysteries. We've all known Bonnie would share in Greg's estate in spite of the way Sylvia behaved. Don't let Bart's wild tales frighten you. If anyone doesn't treat you right, come to me. Greg's away so much, and so busy. You've met all the family, haven't you?"

"No—there seem to be several we haven't met. I didn't even know there was you! And who is the mongoloid boy with the dog?"

"That's Carl," Clay said, his voice suddenly cold. "He's the Morton's retarded son. He won't bother you if you keep your distance."

"I'm not afraid of him! But I'd like to know who was inside and let the dog loose."

He smiled indulgently and reached over to pat her hand. "I'm sure you're mistaken about that. Carl's usually there alone. Mancho probably gave an extra hard jerk when he saw you, and broke the tether. We really should get rid of the beast, I guess—but he's the poor kid's pet."

The road they followed had swung around a few curves, skirting the forest before it crossed a meadow. In less time than Anise could believe, they stopped in front of the tall old house.

Mrs. Morton met them at the door. "Where have you been?" she charged, glowering at Anise. "When we couldn't find you on the beach we were afraid—" She swung her sharp gaze to Clay. "You can tell your brother I won't be responsible for—"

"Now, now, Cousin Fannie," he broke in, patting her shoulder. "Don't race your motor. I found 'em and brought 'em home safe. But I'm going to speak to George about that dog!" He turned to Anise. "Why don't you and Bonnie go to your rooms and rest until dinner. You've had a pretty rugged time."

As they climbed the stairs Anise heard Mrs. Morton say with a snort, "I'm not *your* cousin—and you have nothing to say about Mancho as long as Mr. Greg says Carl can have him. When's Mr. Greg coming home?"

Anise and Bonnie reached their own door while Clay was explaining why Gregory had to stay at the mill at least another day. In her room, with her door closed, Anise could still hear Mrs. Morton's angry protests and Clay's placating answers. She could distinguish only a few of the words, enough to sense that the housekeeper was objecting to their presence here. Why? She wondered. Was it because of extra work and responsibility? Or was she the relative who resented Bonnie on Laura's behalf? Maybe that's why Mr. Morton had seemed unfriendly too. Were they some relation to Laura? Cousins, perhaps?

A couple of hours later when the dinner gong sounded, they went down to the cheerfully lighted breakfast room to find places set for six. Clay was over by the windows, talking to Laura. A stern, bone-thin woman stood behind the child, her neutral-colored hair cut as short as a man's, her features sharp and unattractive. Clay paused in the middle of a sentence and turned to Anise.

"Ah, here we are," he said genially. "Miss Weston, I understand you and Bonnie still haven't met Greg's other daughter, Laura. And this is her governess, Miss Enid Parsons."

Anise smiled at the little girl. She looked almost the same age as Bonnie, but there was little resemblance. Her long straight hair was taffy blonde, her eyes shadowy green, her face plump and lightly freckled. The children gazed at each other in awkward silence, Bonnie more shy than eager as she leaned against Anise. It was hard to fathom Laura's expression. A mixture of smugness, curiosity, and caution that gave her face an unchildlike appearance, and there was suspicion—maybe even malice—in the depths of the grayish-green eyes. Was it more than sibling jealousy?

"You children will have fun playing together now," Clay was saying fatuously when a stocky young man walked into the room. Rather attractive, he had an air of strength and vigor, his wavy blond hair cut in a mod style, his sideburns pale gold against his tanned cheeks.

"Miss Weston, this is Laura's uncle, Bart Graham," Clay said, moving from the window. "I believe you've already met, but not officially."

"Officiously is a better term for the way I accosted her,"

37

Bart said. "I'd forgotten they were coming, and thought we had some more tourist trespassers." His smile at Anise was disarming. "I hope I'm forgiven?"

"Of course," she agreed. "I can understand your wanting to keep trespassers away."

He moved quickly to hold her chair then sat down beside her while Clay seated the others and rang for Deirdre to serve them.

"It's Greg's idea to prohibit trespassing," Bart said, and she couldn't help noting the interest in his eyes as he studied her. In her black dress with its white satin collar, her hair brushed until it gleamed, a touch of makeup to highlight her eyes, she knew she was more attractive than she had been at the beach this afternoon. He was too, for that matter.

"Greg's the boss," he went on pleasantly. "For myself, I'd love to have the beach decorated with trespassers like you. Do you ever go scuba diving?"

"No, and I should think it would be dangerous on a rugged coast like this."

"Not if you know your business and watch the tides," he said.

"Bart loves danger anyway," Clay chimed in from across the table. The two men faced each other, with Anise and Bonnie at one side, Miss Enid and Laura at the other. The children gave each other surreptitious glances, but said nothing.

For a while the table conversation centered on Bart's diving. "He reads adventure tales as well as detective yarns," Clay said, winking at Anise, "and hopes to find a sunken ship full of treasure."

"No such luck," Bart sighed, "but it's exciting to be down among the fish. I catch bigger ones, you notice, then George gets from the surface."

"There was another diver with you," Anise remarked. "Does he live here too?"

"Well, not right here. He—"

"That was Carl," Clay cut in. "The boy you saw at the cottage this afternoon."

Bart turned to her sharply. "What were you doing at the cottage? Didn't anybody warn you about the dog? Mancho is Carl's protector, as well as his pal. He's been taught to attack strangers."

"So I notice!" Anise charged, meeting his concerned gaze,

38

trying to analyze his expression. "Someone in the cottage let the dog loose to attack *us!*"

Bart swung his gaze across the table to Clay who glared right back. "Don't look at me!" Clay snapped. "I was still up in the air, circling for a landing. If you weren't there I suggest you do a little checking, and see that your Cousin George follows my orders to buy Mancho a stronger chain. Miss Weston also thinks someone shot at her. If it wasn't a poacher—well, you and George are the only ones around here who go hunting."

Bart turned to Anise, looking distressed. "Surely you don't think I'd take pot shots at you and Bonnie! In spite of the way I talked on the beach, I think it's wonderful that you both are here. Laura will have someone to play with, and I—" He grinned. "You're the nicest thing that's happened to this God-forsaken place since I came here!"

When they all left the table after dinner, Laura approached Bonnie with an air of nonchalance and said, "I've got a play-house in my room. Want to come and play?"

Bonnie shrank against Anise, glancing up at her questioningly.

"Would you like to go?" Anise asked. Surely she would be safe enough with another little girl and this prim-looking governess, and it would be nice for them to become friends.

"Of course she would," Clay said. "They'll have fun together. Miss Enid, how about looking after both children for a while? I'd like to talk to Anise."

He took her arm and led her to the living room where a small fire scarcely warmed the damp air. "What a skimpy blaze!" he complained, going over to add logs from a hammered-copper basket. "I don't know why old George is so stingy with the wood. There's plenty of it around, he has a good power saw to cut it up, and has trained that idiot son to use it."

"Don't call him an idiot!" Anise protested, her fervor aroused as always by sympathy for the unfortunate. "That makes him sound hopeless!"

Clay threw another chunk of wood on the fire before answering. His expression was curious as he turned to her. "What makes you think he *isn't* hopeless?"

"I've worked with retarded children as a teacher's aide, and I found that in most cases their condition isn't hopeless at all if

39

they're treated with kindness and understanding. They can be educated to the point of living useful lives—like Carl learning to use the power saw. Why is he living in an isolated place like this? Who looks after him?"

"His mother, mostly." Clay poked at the logs which were beginning to smoke, as if damp.

"His mother?" Was it Mrs. Morton who had released the dog this afternoon? She obviously resented their presence here.

"Oh, George helps too, of course, and that's part of Bart's job here, but about all he has taught Carl is to skin dive. Probably with the hope that he'll get confused underwater and drown himself."

"Oh, no!" she cried, then saw that he was teasing.

"Okay, let's say he taught Carl because he needed a buddy. It isn't safe to dive alone, especially where the tides are strong. Bart's nuts about scuba diving and no one else around here would join him."

He sobered and pulled a chair over to sit close and regard her quizzically. "You really feel for Carl, the poor guy, don't you? Most people turn their faces away with a shudder. It would be a blessing if you'd make friends with him, since you've had experience along that line. He looks repulsive, but he's a gentle sort of goof—I don't think he'd ever hurt you."

"Of course he wouldn't! I don't think he's repulsive, either. Just—well, different. I've found mongoloids very responsive to any friendly overture, and they need lots of love."

He was grinning again and his eyes sparkled with amusement. "Go easy on the love stuff! Physically Carl's almost nineteen, even though his mental age is hardly seven. Show him any affection and he might get ideas you wouldn't like. Retarded or not, he's still all male, and you're a very attractive female. Another word of caution—don't trust that dog Mancho for a second if Carl isn't there to control him. He's getting so vicious I'm afraid to be around him myself."

Anise shuddered. "Maybe he wouldn't be so cross if he weren't tied up. I've heard—"

Clay shook his head. "That big mutt was born cross. I don't know why Greg lets the boy keep him. Not because he has a soft spot in his heart—that's for sure! If Greg has a soft spot it's in his head!"

Anise gazed at him in wonder and some dismay. His face looked as harsh and bitter as his voice had suddenly become.

Seeing her expression, his own softened with a rueful smile. "I shouldn't talk that way about my brother—is that what you're thinking? But he has done so many damned outlandish things. Oh well, let's talk about something pleasant for a change. You, for instance."

She shook her head. "I'd like to know more about Carl. Has he been to a special school for the mentally retarded?"

"Oh, sure. His parents hid him in an institution, ashamed to have him around; they claimed it was hard on Deirdre. I suppose he had all the schooling he could absorb, but the teachers nagged George to keep him home at least part of the time."

"It is better. The school where I worked provided bus service and encouraged living at home, as affording a more normal life. How would you like to spend your life in an institution?"

Again he grinned, his eyebrows arched over his hooded eyes. "I wouldn't! And I wouldn't like to spend the evening talking about Carl either. Let's step outside and see if more fog has rolled in." He caught her hand and pulled her to her feet.

Outside the tangy salt air was fresh and moist, so little fog that only a light film of mist diffused the moonlight. "I'm glad we're having nice weather while you are here," Clay said. "I suppose you'll leave in a week or two, when Bonnie feels at home?"

"Oh no! I was asked to stay all summer!" Seeing the startled look on his face, she went on urgently, "It's really important that I do. Bonnie's so shy and insecure, and has been through a bad experience losing her mother. I wouldn't dare leave her!"

There was something grim about his brief silence as he studied her in the dim glow of the moon. Then he smiled and took her hand again, murmuring, "I see. Well, let's go down to the beach. The tide should be out again now."

He guided her steps along the garden path. As they reached the stairs he steadied her with an arm about her waist. She tried not to be self-conscious about his encircling arm. It did help, for the stairs were uneven and the filtered moonlight did little to make them visible. Remembering the way Laura had come running down these steps to meet Bart, she asked, "Is Bart Graham supposed to help with Laura's care as well as Carl's?"

"Not particularly," he replied and there was coldness in his voice again. "He's here mostly to help his cousins take care of Melanie."

"Melanie?"

"That's Greg's wife—Bart's sister. You'll meet her as soon as she's well enough to be presentable. I suppose Sylvia didn't tell you much about the family. We heard she had banished Greg from her life, and Bonnie's, completely. I wish to God —" He broke off as they reached the foot of the stairs.

"Look here," he said, taking her gently by the shoulders to face her in the pale moonlight. "I make it a point not to discuss my brother's affairs with anyone. It upsets him to no end if he finds I've said too much, so I try to say nothing. Now, let's talk about you. I understand you're a nurse?"

"Not an RN. I couldn't afford the training."

As they sat on the cool dry sand and she told him a little about her younger brothers and sisters and her father's painful accident at his work as machinist, which forced her to abandon her plans for either a college degree or a hospital diploma. She had taken the brief LVN course at City College while working part time as teachers' aide.

"It sounds gruelling," he commented. "Don't you ever have any fun?"

"Of course, and I've had a few dates." Then she added honestly, "But not very many."

He picked up her hand and began to play with her fingers, sending tingles of excitement up her arm. "I'll bet that wasn't for lack of invitations! I'd love to take you dancing myself. Some evening let's turn Bonnie over to Miss Enid and fly our plane to San Francisco for a big night out. How about it?"

She laughed, delighted with the idea. "I've never flown to a dance! It would be great fun!"

Suddenly she was conscience-smitten and scrambled to her feet. "I've left Bonnie too long. She's painfully shy and doesn't quite feel at home here yet. I must get back to the house."

He was on his feet beside her. "Miss Enid will take good care of her. She's the soul of responsibility—but no fun at all. Look at that moon!"

It was brighter now, and seemed bigger. He moved close, his arm curving lightly about her. She felt he was being a little too intimate, yet it would seem rude to object when the intimacy had only a friendly, sheltering air—nothing at which to take offense. She stood there feeling warm and protected until a cloud blew across the moon, leaving the sky black. His arm drew her closer.

"We must go," she said, breathless with a sharp feeling that he meant to kiss her. She wasn't ready for that—she hardly knew him!

He released her promptly, then caught her hand again as they plodded through the deep sand to the stairs. She didn't need his arm to steady her on the way up, but it was nice having him near, ready to help if she should stumble in the dark. It was windy now at the top of the cliff, and he took her arm to guide her through the darkness of the garden. Again the contact gave her a pleasant, sheltered feeling—along with a throb of romance far more stimulating.

There was no one inside the dim entrance hall. Keeping hold of her arm, Clay gazed down at her, his expression unfathomable as he moaned, "I wish you hadn't come here, Anise—dammit!"

"But why?" she gasped. Why was everyone so concerned about their being here—as if they were in the way, or something terrible might happen to them! "What's wrong with our being here?"

She could feel his tension mount as his grip tightened on her arm. "It's just that you're so damned sweet. Anywhere else, under different circumstances, it would be wonderful knowing you, having fun together, but. . . ." The pause lengthened as he drew a sharp breath and released her arm. His voice returned to a casual tone as he said, "Miss Enid has probably taken Bonnie back to her room. Be careful of the child—she means a lot to us now that she's one of the family."

He cradled her hand in his palms as they reached the foot of the stairs. For a moment he seemed about to say more, then almost curtly he told her good-night and vanished down the dark hallway.

Anise slowly climbed the stairs to her room, troubled and apprehensive. Had Clay been trying to warn her about something here, just as Mr. Morton had—and Mrs. Morton too, though less directly? Bart's warning had been quite explicit, yet Clay called it hogwash. What was the matter with this place!

Her anxiety increased as she went through her room to Bonnie's, switching on lights, and found Bonnie wasn't there. Thinking she must still be with Laura and Miss Enid, she went back into the hall, walking past several doors, listening for the sound of voices. Beyond the last door the hall turned, and this section was even dimmer than the first. Hardly a sound could be heard except for faint rustlings that had no significance. Her pulse began to race with rising uneasiness—she felt as if the old house had swallowed Bonnie. Should she call out, or go downstairs and hunt for Deirdre or Mrs. Morton . . . .

Her heart caught on a painful beat at a swishing sound directly behind her, accompanied by rapid footsteps. Before she could turn to see who or what it was, she was clutched in a tight, viselike grip that pinned her arms to her sides. The only sound now was the heavy panting of someone at her shoulder. She felt a scream rise to her throat, but couldn't find her voice at all. The sudden fright numbed her limbs and made the hallway turn completely black as she felt herself fainting away.

CHAPTER 5

"Don't, Sylvia! Don't tell him! I'll make it up to you!"

It was a woman's hysterical voice sobbing in her ear, and Anise recovered her waning senses. She could cope with a woman. Regaining her strength, she twisted sharply and freed herself from the clutching arms. Turning, she faced a wraith-like figure—a pale slender woman with long disheveled blonde hair. A white filmy robe added to her spectral appearance in the dusky corridor.

"You're not Sylvia!" the woman quavered, staring at her. "You're *real*!"

Before Anise could answer, Deirdre came rushing around the corner of the hallway to take the woman in a strong grip. "I'm sorry, Miss Weston," she panted. "I only left her for a minute. I didn't know—" She broke off to quiet the woman who had started to struggle. "Come on, Melanie, we must go back to your room—it's time for your medicine, remember?"

Anise watched as the two women went into one of the rooms and closed the door. In her confusion she had forgotten to ask Deirdre where to find Bonnie. She headed for the door, her hand raised to knock, then stopped short.

Somewhere in the house somebody screamed—a thin, wailing shriek of terror. It sounded like a child—it sounded like Bonnie!

Anise rushed back down the hall, around the turn to the hall that led to her room and Bonnie's. Miss Enid was standing behind Laura at the dumbwaiter opening, both of them peering down. Bonnie's screams were coming from the shaft.

"Bonnie!" Anise cried, rushing to the door. Miss Enid and Laura turned to her, startled.

"She fell!" Laura cried. "She just opened the door and tumbled down the hole!"

"She must have thought that was the door to her room," Miss Enid said shakily, reaching for the pulley rope. "She didn't fall far—the cage was down on first, and she's here on top of it."

Peering in, Anise saw Bonnie eight or nine feet below, beginning to rise as Miss Enid pulled the rope. Glancing upward, she saw that the shaft extended up into unfathomable darkness.

"Is there another story above this?" she asked.

"Yes—it's the Morton's apartment." Miss Enid's voice had a breathless sound as she added, "It's a good thing the cage wasn't up there. Bonnie could have dropped clear to the bottom—and if she jerked the ropes on her fall they might have brought the cage down on top of her."

Bonnie was sobbing as she came to door level and flung her arms around Anise. "Laura pushed me! She pushed me in!"

"I did not!" Laura cried. "When she opened the door I tried to grab her so she *wouldn't* fall—but she was already falling!"

"That's right," Miss Enid said nervously. "Bonnie's naughty to say such a thing about her sister! Laura loves having her here!"

Anise carried Bonnie to her own room, sat on the bed and held her until the child's sobs gradually quieted.

"She scared me!" Bonnie whimpered when Anise questioned her about the fall. "I was running away from Laura because she scared me!"

"How?" Anise asked, still holding the trembling child close.

"She kept talking about horrible things that happen in the forest. I had told her about the big bird grabbing that cute little squirrel, and she said that was nothing. She said there were monsters—and fire comes out of their noses—and they eat you alive!"

"You don't believe that, do you, darling?"

"Well, maybe not, but it scared me—the way she told it. So I ran and thought I'd come to our door, and she was chasing me—and when I opened the door she pushed me!"

"Maybe she just accidentally bumped into you. She said she tried to grab you to keep you from falling," Anise reminded her. Probably Bonnie's terror made it feel as if she had been pushed when she lost her balance.

"I don't care what she says!" Bonnie declared, getting to her feet. "I don't like her much. I don't see why I have to have a sister! Mother didn't tell me I had one."

"You have different mothers, so you're half sisters. Maybe she hasn't played with children much and doesn't know how, but after you get used to each other—"

"I don't think I'm going to like my father, either," Bonnie broke in, her mouth tight in her pale little face.

"Let's not make up your mind about him yet, dear—you haven't even met him."

"My mother hated him, and Laura says he's mean—she likes Uncle Clay better."

"Well, that's her privilege, but you shouldn't adopt her opinion of your father." Glancing down at Bonnie's knees she saw that they were scratched and bleeding. "Oh Bonnie, you hurt yourself! Let's get the first-aid kit."

As she dressed the minor wounds, Anise assured herself that Laura and Enid were no doubt right. In her fear, Bonnie had thought she was pushed, but it would be easy to lose her balance if she expected the door to open to her own room. It was unlikely that Laura would push her, for, as Miss Enid said, she should be delighted to have another child to play with in this isolated spot. And she was too young to worry about the division of their father's estate, if, indeed, she knew anything about it at all.

Anise was helping Bonnie get ready for bed when Deirdre knocked and came into the room. "I hope Melanie didn't scare you," she told Anise. "I wasn't supposed to leave her alone—Mom and Bart both went to the cottage and asked me to stay with her. I thought she was asleep—I only meant to be gone a minute so I didn't lock the door. But you never know what she'll do when she's having one of her bad spells. I hope—I mean . . . ." She clasped her hands together nervously. "If you

47

wouldn't say anything to Mom or anyone about my leaving her. . . ."

"I won't say anything," Anise promised, anxious to end the girl's obvious uneasiness. As Deirdre ducked out, thanking her profusely, Anise surmised that Mrs. Morton must be pretty strict with her. Was she in complete charge of the household? Normally Melanie would be in charge, wouldn't she? As Gregory's wife she should be mistress of the mansion. What were these "bad spells" she had? Periods of insanity? Why had Melanie been so terrified on mistaking her for Sylvia? "Don't tell him!" she had cried.

Pondering it all, Anise once again had trouble getting to sleep. At some time during the night she heard the plane take off, circle overhead, then drone into the distance. Clay must have left, and that intensified her uneasiness. Somehow he seemed to offer more protection than anyone else here. Yet— protection against what? Against their being shot at, or being attacked by the dog? Against Bonnie falling down the dumbwaiter shaft? She wanted to tell him about that—see what he had to say.

The more she thought over the day's experiences, the more she began to believe this wasn't a safe or happy home for Bonnie. When the wind began to blow harder, whistling around turrets and cupolas, she gave up trying to sleep, and got up to write a letter to the Dimmicks, telling them everything that had happened. Then she wondered how she would mail it.

Toward morning she heard the plane circle and land. If Clay were returning, she could ask him to mail her letter next time he flew back to civilization.

She was sleeping soundly when a light touch on her cheek dragged her out of a dream. Bonnie was gazing at her, still in her pajamas, her brown hair tousled.

"That bell rang again, Miss Weston. Does it mean breakfast?"

"Oh dear!" Anise sat up and tried to rub the sleep from her eyes. What had she been dreaming about? Something frustrating, but, though it had been vivid while she was dreaming, she couldn't remember any coherent details now. She threw back the covers and crossed the room to open the draperies. The sea was bright aquamarine, sparkling with whitecaps in brilliant sunshine. The wind whipped lightly through the trees. It must have blown the fog away.

"See what a beautiful day it is!" she exclaimed, calling Bonnie over to share her enjoyment of the scene.

Deirdre knocked and poked her head in at the door. "The bell means breakfast in half an hour. Mr. Gregory flew in before dawn so we'll be getting back to our regular routine now."

She disappeared, and Anise stared at the closed door, wishing her pulse wouldn't race at the thought of meeting Gregory Lockwood again. She glanced down at Bonnie whose little face mirrored her own uneasiness.

"Maybe everything will be better now with your daddy home," she said, struggling for a tone of assurance. "Let's hurry and dress so we can go down to meet him."

"No!" Bonnie shrank back, eyes wide and fearful. "I don't want to see my daddy! My mother and Laura both said—"

"Look, darling," Anise sat down and drew the child close, "your mother and daddy quarreled and parted, but that doesn't mean he's bad, or doesn't love you. Maybe they just quit loving each other, the way people do sometimes. And you mustn't take Laura's opinion as your own. Let's get acquainted with him so you can make up your own mind. I promise that if you're not happy here I'll take you to live with your grandparents."

"No! I don't want to live with them either. I just want to live with you! Can't we go somewhere together?"

Anise hugged the child and found her trembling. "I love you too, Bonnie," she said, "and I might be able to manage somehow. But first, you must try to love your daddy—do your very best! You may find you like him a lot better than you expect. At least, give him a fair chance."

She dressed the child in a pink jumper over a demure little blouse, brushed the brown hair until it shone with bronze lights, then added a band of pink ribbon. Wearing a plain dark dress herself, she took Bonnie's hand as they went down to the breakfast room.

Gregory was alone, standing at the windows, his back to them. He turned slowly, and Anise had the same strange emotions that she had the stormy night when he came to see Sylvia —the same fascination, the same sense of his authority, stern and unyielding, as if he would always be in full command of any situation in which he found himself. He didn't seem quite as tall or dark-haired as he had that night, for there was the

49

identical bronze sheen to his hair that she had brushed into Bonnie's. His eyes were as she remembered—deep set and dark below shading eyelids and slanted brows, but his mouth looked kinder now, especially when he gazed down at Bonnie and smiled.

"So you're my little girl," he said. "I hope you'll be happy here. If there's anything you want, just tell me."

Bonnie didn't answer, simply gazed up at him and shrank closer to Anise. His smile faded as he studied her another moment, then he shrugged.

"It may take a while," he said, turning to Anise. "No telling what Sylvia has told her—probably made me sound like a monster." He shrugged again, as if dismissing the subject, and said, "I want you to know, Miss Weston, how much I appreciate your bringing Bonnie here. I'm sorry I couldn't be here to welcome you, but we've had labor problems at the mill. Are your rooms satisfactory?"

"They're lovely!" Anise declared. He had pulled out a chair for her at the table, so she sat down and watched as he drew one out for Bonnie, who still hovered close to her. "Go sit down, honey," Anise murmured in her ear, but the child held back.

"Come take your seat, Bonnie," he said, and when she still hesitated, he added more firmly, "I'm waiting."

As if Bonnie felt it too, that air of authority that couldn't be defied, she moved slowly to the chair, her head tilted to gaze up at him. When he had seated her, she turned wide, questioning eyes to Anise. Anise smiled, but there was no answering smile on the child's face, only deep anxiety. What had Sylvia told her about him? Anise wondered.

"Clay says you have already done some exploring around Mendolair," Gregory said after Deirdre had served them. "There are many interesting places to discover, but I hope you've learned your lesson about wandering into the woods without a guide."

She met his gaze steadily. "Did Clay tell you that someone shot at us, after turning the dog loose on us?"

He frowned. "You don't think that was deliberate, do you? I've told George to post more 'no-hunting' signs, and to chain Mancho to a spike set firmly in the ground. Actually you were in no danger from the dog as long as Carl was near. It's rather

50

wonderful, the rapport that has developed between that retarded boy and his pet. And Carl is a gentle, harmless person."

"I know," she agreed, and was rewarded by a smile that changed his expression completely.

"That's right—Clay says you're very sympathetic and understanding about the boy. I appreciate that. Melanie—"

He glanced thoughtfully out the window. For a moment she thought he wasn't going to continue, then he said in a guarded tone, "I'm sorry Melanie wasn't well enough to give you a hostess's welcome. You'll have to excuse her for the time being, but one of these days I'll take you up to meet her."

She was about to reply that she had met Melanie last night, then she remembered Deirdre's distress about it, and decided not to risk getting the girl in trouble.

"I'm impressed with this rugged coast," she said in an effort to change the subject. "But isn't it lonely for the family—being so isolated?"

His smile was a bit grim. "Maybe—but there's compensation in being away from the mad rush of cities and freeways. We want you to enjoy Mendolair, but to be safe there are a few precautions you should take—such as not wandering into the woods. The surf isn't safe for swimming, either—at least not without a strong swimmer on hand. Bonnie shouldn't even wade knee deep, for the strong tides plow unexpected holes in the sand where a child could suddenly drop to a depth over her head, and the undertow can be vicious. Don't wander away from the cove that gives access to the stairs. There are other coves beyond rocky points, but if the tide caught you in one of them you'd be trapped."

He turned to Bonnie who was gazing at him anxiously and hadn't touched her food. "I'm not trying to frighten you, dear. There are plenty of safe, interesting things to do around here, especially on a nice day like this. Shall we go down to the beach after breakfast and see if we can find a pink or lavender sea anemone in one of the tide pools?"

Bonnie shook her head, solemn and round-eyed as a little owl. Drawing a deep breath, he tried again, as if determined to make friends with his daughter. "Your Uncle Clay says you met your half sister yesterday. Did you enjoy playing with Laura?"

Again Bonnie shook her head, saying nothing. Gregory studied her for a moment, gave her a bleak smile and said,

"You'd better eat your breakfast, hon. You haven't touched a bite."

Anise and Gregory had finished their breakfast and were having a second cup of coffee before Bonnie, at Anise's gentle urging, ate a little cereal. Before long she pushed her dish away and said she wasn't hungry.

"No use forcing it," Gregory said, getting up to draw their chairs back. "Let's take a walk. I want to show you a path where it should be safe to wander as far as you like, with no danger of getting lost or being shot at, and Mancho is never allowed that far from the cottage without Carl to control him —preferably on leash."

They went out the front door, through the garden to a side gate so overgrown with ivy that Anise hadn't noticed it before. They had just passed through, Bonnie clinging to Anise's hand, when Gregory stopped and looked back. Miss Enid and Laura had come from the house and were hurrying toward them.

"Daddy! Daddy!" Laura cried, running to him with hands outstretched to be swept up in his arms. Watching the child give him a fervent hug, Anise wondered if she had greeted Clay as eagerly. She had given Bonnie an unfavorable impression of their father, saying she loved Clay best, yet she was kicking her heels in obvious delight now as she cried, "Why didn't you let us know you were home? We'd have come down to breakfast with you!"

Gregory was beaming as he put her down and tousled her hair fondly, his face lighted in a way that made him look almost like a different person.

"We're going on a picnic!" Laura said. "Will you come too? And Bonnie? Mrs. Morton packed us a lunch in a basket with fried chicken and little pink cupcakes!"

He glanced inquiringly at Miss Enid who moistened her lips, looking strangely uneasy as she said, "We were just going to the little park up beyond the point. I'm afraid that Bonnie wouldn't want—"

"Of course she wants to come!" Laura cried, grabbing Bonnie's hand, her plump, freckled face alight. "We have nuts to feed the squirrels—they eat right out of your hand! You want to come, don't you? Please!"

Bonnie didn't look as if she were being invited to a picnic. The wide anxious eyes darting from Laura to Gregory and back again, gave her an air of having to choose between two

52

evils. Anise felt oddly repelled by Laura's enthusiasm too, even though it sounded genuine. Recalling the way Bonnie had been frightened last night, she said, "I think Bonnie had better stay with me."

"No—let her go," Gregory said, his tone austere again. "Miss Enid can take care of them both—she'll soon start tutoring Bonnie along with Laura, and this will give the three of them a good chance to get acquainted. Besides, I want to talk to you."

Anise was watching Laura and Miss Enid who were gazing at each other in some sort of private communication, Laura looking stubborn, Miss Enid frightened. Whatever the silent battle was about, Laura must have won it, for Miss Enid's shoulders slumped a little as she turned to Bonnie and said, "Come on, dear. We'd love to have you."

Still with grave misgivings, Anise let Bonnie go. She watched the three cross the garden to a gate at the other side which led to a path not far from the top of the cliff. Bonnie looked small and vulnerable, lagging a little behind Miss Enid while Laura skipped blithely ahead. Yet it was silly to worry about her. Surely she was safe enough with another little girl and her governess.

"She'll be all right," Gregory said, and Anise turned to find him studying her with speculation that gave his dark brown eyes the same flash of amber that often lighted Bonnie's eyes.

"I—I suppose so. I guess you're sure Miss Enid can be trusted?"

His mouth tightened with a look of annoyance. "Would I let her take care of Laura if I thought she couldn't be trusted? What makes you so suspicious? Did Sylvia poison your mind too?"

"It has nothing to do with Sylvia! It was what happened last night right here!" She told him about Bonnie's accident at the dumbwaiter shaft, ending, "Bonnie said Laura pushed her!"

His countenance darkened. "That's ridiculous! Laura? She has always been one of the sweetest, most amenable and affectionate children I've ever known. I can't imagine her harming anyone—especially not Bonnie! She's been looking forward eagerly to having a sister to play with. I expect Bonnie stumbled as she opened the door, then saw the dark shaft below and was so terrified she didn't know what happened afterward."

Anise had to admit that her common sense told her the

53

same thing. She sighed as she added candidly, "Laura insists that she tried to grab Bonnie to keep her from falling, and Miss Enid backs her up."

"That's more like it!" he declared. "At the moment Laura's a more lovable child than Bonnie, but I'm hoping that when Bonnie gets used to us—gets over the fear her mother wickedly instilled in her—when she learns to love us—"

They walked together along the path. After a brooding moment he shrugged in the way that often presaged a change of mood, and said, "Laura will be good for her. Laura's so outgoing and uncomplicated, she'll bring her out of that shell."

He smiled and took her hand as they headed toward a grove of trees. "We'll tour the grounds first, then I'll show you a trail where you and Bonnie will be perfectly safe. It skirts the forest, wanders through green meadows, safely back from the cliff yet with a frequent sweeping view of the ocean."

She began to breathe easier, for with his hand cradling hers, his gold-flecked brown eyes holding her gaze, she could almost lay her fears to rest. At the moment he seemed exactly the father Bonnie needed, and this green wooded shore above the blue sea was an ideal place to spend the summer. Yet, somewhere deep within her, below the sense of security he fostered, there was still a churning uneasiness that would not be quieted.

CHAPTER 6

Anise was more impressed than ever with Mendolair as Gregory led her over winding, fern-banked paths in a garden bright with gladioli, snapdragons, and many flowers she couldn't identify at a glance.

"This looks as if it had been planted right in the middle of the forest!" she exclaimed, marveling at the low, symmetrical beds of plants in vivid shades of blue and orange, lavender and magenta.

"It was," he replied, seeming pleased with her admiration. "A retired nurseryman cleared out enough rain forest and peat bog to indulge his passion for gardening. He didn't disturb the wild flowers around the edges, though it's a little late for them now. Some of the plantings have spread all over, especially those forget-me-nots. George doesn't have time for much cultivating, Clay's busy at the mill, and Bart would rather go skin diving. We're training Carl to take care of the gardens but he still needs supervision."

"It's beautiful just as it is," she declared, following the mossy path, enjoying the pattern of golden sunlight that penetrated the leafy branches arched overhead.

"This is one of the reasons I bought Mendolair," he said, coming up beside her as the path widened. "The whole Mendocino coast is fascinating to me. It's a conglomeration of everything. Gentle green pastures and almost impenetrable forests. A rugged, rocky coastline alternating with sunny coves and sandy beaches. The towns are a mixture of mod art and sophisticated cultural centers, sandwiched between old-timers living in mid-Victorian houses, even more gingerbreadish than mine."

"You sound like the Chamber of Commerce," she teased, and he laughed. Then a shadow crossed his face.

"I can't help wanting all the household to love the place as I do. Some don't, but I hope you and Bonnie will."

The meandering path eventually brought them back to the house and the smaller buildings behind it. He showed her the generator that occupied one of the sheds and provided their electricity. He led her uphill to a sparkling blue reservoir enclosed by a chain link fence.

"That's our water supply," he said. "It's piped from two cold bubbling springs. The fence is to keep two-legged as well as four-legged animals from wading into it."

She glanced up at him and thought how different he seemed from the austere, brooding man who had visited Sylvia that stormy night. The dappled sunlight brightened the bronze gleam of his hair and softened the sharpness of his features. Yet there was still the air of authority which was so much a part of him. She thought of the mill and lumber interests under his command, as well as this extraordinary estate which he obviously loved.

"Were the generator and reservoir here when you bought Mendolair?" she asked.

He grinned. "Lord, no! The house was completely rustic. Not even a bathroom, let alone any wiring. There was an attempt at central heating with a wood furnace, but it was pretty ineffectual in winter. I've added all the modern improvements."

"Including a butane furnace." Anise remembered what the housekeeper had said. "Mrs. Morton seems afraid it might explode."

He shrugged. "I had to warn her and George it's explosive, of course. I also told them it's quite safe if they'll follow instructions. They're old-timers, a bit skeptical of modern improvements. But when I asked if they'd like to go back to kero-

56

sene lamps, outhouses and continuously chopping wood, they decided the jeopardy was justified by the convenience."

He led her beyond the reservoir to a well-marked trail through the woods. "You can follow this path anytime you want to take Bonnie for a walk," he said. "There's no maze of crisscross trails to confuse you, like those in the forest where you got lost. Just stick to the path, and avoid the few danger spots I'll point out."

Before long they emerged from the woods onto a long green meadow that extended to the cliffs above the ocean. Cattle browsed or slept, or waded and drank from a shallow stream that meandered over moss and pebbles to disappear in the little gully that split the cliff.

"There's a small waterfall there, but don't go near it," he said. "The ground is slippery, and if you skidded into the gully the water might carry you down into one of the rockiest, most dangerous coves along the coast. Keep Bonnie well back in the meadow. Along here, you'd better not leave the path at all."

They crossed the shallow stream on a row of flat rocks, and followed a trail into another forest that spilled down the side of a steep mountain. The tall columns of redwood and fir were close together now, bringing semidarkness. There was deep quiet except for an occasional birdsong in the treetops, and the distant roar of the ocean.

Anise found herself very much aware of Gregory's presence close beside her. It occurred to her she couldn't be near him at any time without being stirred by some emotion, either fear, distrust, admiration, or a strange feeling she hadn't yet been able to identify. Her heart was thumping almost painfully by the time they left the shadowy forest and came to a round, framework gazebo perched on a rocky promontory at the edge of the cliff.

He touched her arm to guide her up the steps into the gazebo, and her breath seemed to stop completely on the gasp that caught in her throat.

From this height she could see both directions along the rugged coastline with its coves and promontories. The ocean lay peaceful except for the bursts of foam wherever it surged against the scattered rocks thrust up in the surf. Along the top of the cliff, between the forest and the drop-off, wild flowers bloomed in patches of red, yellow, and purple.

"Do you see why I love it here?" Gregory asked, his tone al-

57

most reverent. Then it hardened as he added, "But in spite of its beauty, this coast can be harsh and cruel."

He paused, then went on thoughtfully, "In a way, maybe, the danger adds to the fascination. See that ship making her peaceful way along the horizon? In a storm, the wind and tide could bring her crashing onto the rocks if she drifted too close to shore. In a fog, only the warning of the foghorns can keep her safely away. A person could fall from these high cliffs and be fatally injured on jagged rocks, or washed out to sea. If you bring Bonnie to this gazebo, be sure to keep tight hold of her hand."

Anise shivered a little, and immediately felt his arm curve about her shoulders. "I'm not trying to frighten you," he said gently. "But you must take all my warnings seriously. It can be dangerous here."

"That's what Mr. Morton said the day he brought us from the airport," she told him, stepping away from the warmth of his encircling arm because it evoked too many wild emotions. "Only somehow I gathered that Mr. Morton wasn't thinking about the ruggedness of the coast or the country when he said it wouldn't be safe for Bonnie and me."

Gregory made a sound of derision. "I wouldn't have had you bring her into any unavoidable danger. Sit down, Anise. I'd like to ask a few questions. I hope you'll give me direct answers."

A curved seat was attached to the open framework of the small structure. Gregory waited for her to sit down, then took his place across from her. She was grateful for the four or five feet of wooden flooring between them. She could think better at this distance.

As he seemed to be mentally framing his first question, he gazed at her with the same brooding appraisal that had disquieted her the night he came to see Sylvia. She felt a misty breeze whip a strand of hair across her face, and found her fingers shaky as she brushed it back.

"Tell me about Sylvia. What kind of a mother was she to Bonnie?" He was scowling now, his eyes hooded and hawklike.

"How do I know?" she parried. "I was only with them after she became ill. I'm sure she loved Bonnie very much."

"Or was she simply interested in keeping her away from me? I had partial custody, you know, but they—Sylvia and her parents—convinced me that it upset Bonnie whenever I tried

58

to visit. I could see that myself. I couldn't overcome her fear of me, fear I'm sure they instilled deliberately. So I had to be satisfied with sending money and gifts. Do you know whether or not she ever received them?"

Anise shook her head. "No gifts came while I was there. At least, none I know of."

His eyes were on her meditatively for a few moments before he asked, "How was Sylvia after that night I was there? Did she tell you anything about it?"

"She was upset." Anise thought back to Sylvia's wild weeping. "I remember she said she wouldn't believe you, and you could never have Bonnie. She called you wicked and cruel, and wanted to phone her lawyer in the middle of the night. But the doctor had given her a tranquilizer and—"

"Do you think I'm wicked and cruel?" Gregory demanded, his face tight now, his glance sharp and penetrating.

"I—I don't know you very well yet," she faltered. At this moment she had a feeling that he could be wicked and cruel. Yet less than an hour ago she'd had the warm feeling that he could be trusted, even loved!

He closed his eyes and shook his head, as if to banish a disturbing thought. His expression softened as he drew a deep sigh.

"Tell me about Bonnie's grandparents. The Dimmicks. What was their attitude after Sylvia died?"

Anise was seized with a sharp sense of guilt as she remembered her conference with the Dimmicks after the funeral. They had warned her against Gregory, against this home where he wanted to keep his daughter. They had asked her to gather evidence that it wasn't a suitable place for the child, and that he wasn't a fit guardian. She had been finding such evidence from the moment Mr. Morton started the drive to bring them from the airport. Yet here she was answering questions, as if she could place perfect trust in this man she was warned against.

"The Dimmicks would love to have Bonnie," she replied, her lips feeling tight as she decided that was absolutely all she would say about them or Sylvia.

"They'll never get her!" He ground the words through his teeth. Then, as if sensing her withdrawal and knowing he had pursued the subject as far as he could, he stood up and let his face relax in a smile.

"I have more of Mendolair to show you. Shall we go on?"

The woods became sparse as they followed a trail that widened into the semblance of a road. Presently they arrived at a junction with a rocky road that wound steeply up the mountainside.

"This is the only place where you're in danger of taking a wrong turn." Gregory paused and gestured ahead. "Just be sure to follow the easy, downhill trail. It will bring you out shortly onto another meadow that leads to a beach as safe as any along the coast. That's the end of this trail and my property in that direction. You and Bonnie can go there, but stay out of the water unless a strong swimmer is with you."

Turning back to scowl up at the mountain road, he said, "I don't want you ever to take Bonnie up there, or even go there yourself. The road leads to an abandoned quarry. The steep sides of that quarry are lined with loose gravel and crushed shale that could bury anyone who fell into it. It should be filled in or fenced off, but it doesn't belong to me, and so far I haven't been able to get anything done about it. It's off limits to everyone at Mendolair and I don't want—"

He broke off as a boy and a dog came running around the road which curved down out of the forest. Anise recognized Carl and Mancho.

At sight of Gregory, Carl came to a skidding stop and seemed about to turn and run back up the hill. Mancho came bounding down the road, his sleek, spotted body lithe and menacing, his tongue lolling in the sharp-toothed cavern of his open jaws.

With a cry of alarm, Anise moved instinctively behind Gregory, knowing it would be futile to run. Gregory quickly turned to pull her close with his encircling arm.

"Don't be afraid! Mancho won't hurt you when Carl or I have him under control. He's been taught to attack strangers who show up alone."

By then the dog had almost reached them. Gregory said, "Sit!" in his quiet, authoritative voice, and Mancho came to an abrupt stop on his haunches. He panted and wriggled like a pup as he gazed expectantly up into Gregory's face.

"Good dog," Gregory said, stooping to pat the flat head. "Now Mancho, shake hands with Anise."

Keeping his arm about her, Gregory moved her closer to

the dog. Cautiously, she extended her hand, not at all sure it wouldn't be snapped off by those sharp teeth.

"Shake!" Gregory repeated. Mancho licked his chops, sniffed her outstretched hand, then obediently lifted his paw. She took it gingerly, then as Mancho wriggled closer, his dark eyes as eager as those of any ordinary dog, she reached out and scratched his head.

"You're friends now," Gregory said. "But don't try to handle him alone yet, and keep Bonnie away from him until she has a chance to get acquainted with him while one of us is around."

Carl had been coming slowly down the hill, his head hanging. He stood before Gregory looking like a child who expected to be whipped.

"You know better than to go up that road, Carl." Gregory's voice was stern again, yet there was an underlying gentleness as an expression of tender sadness softened his features.

Carl made a gutteral sound of assent, ducking his head to watch his foot as he scuffed it over a rocky spot in the road.

"Then why did you go there? Can't I trust you anymore?"

Carl glanced up in alarm. "Mancho! It was Mancho! I went after Mancho!"

Something like amusement twinkled in Gregory's dark eyes, but his mouth was still stern. "Don't blame Mancho. He does whatever you tell him to. You're supposed to keep him with you, and you know you could have kept him away from the quarry road. I don't want to have to send a steam shovel up there to dig your bodies out of the gravel someday. Don't ever go up there again! Do you understand?"

Carl nodded, his flat-lidded eyes shot with worry. "Never! Never!" he repeated.

"All right, Carl. I'll trust you once more. Now I want to ask you something about the other day when Mancho tried to attack Miss Weston and my little girl at your cottage. I'm glad you were there in time to stop him. But I want to know who was inside and turned Mancho loose."

Carl seemed to shrink down into his sweater. Panic narrowed his eyes. "B-b-broke!" he sputtered, his voice more gutteral than ever. "Mancho b-b-broke loose!"

"I can hardly believe that, Carl." Gregory was again being gentle with the boy. "Someone was there. Someone was shooting, too. So carelessly that Bonnie and Miss Weston could have been hit. Who was it?"

Carl's glance darted about wildly as if looking for escape. His jaw worked, but for a long moment he couldn't say a word. Then the sounds burst forth, spitting from his lips, loud and gutteral, but completely inarticulate. At least, Anise could make nothing at all of the outburst, but Gregory was nodding as if he understood.

"It's all right, Carl, if you're sure you don't know. Nobody's blaming you, so run along. Take Mancho down to the beach for a while if you like. But if you ever find out who was there that afternoon, let me know."

Visibly expanding with relief, Carl whistled to his dog and they both went bounding down the trail toward the beach.

Smiling now, Gregory turned to Anise. "Well, this little episode should mark the quarry trail well enough in your memory so you'll never wander up there in ignorance or by mistake. I'm sure you're too concerned over Bonnie's welfare to take her there deliberately."

"I certainly won't! What on earth was that boy telling you about that day at the cottage?"

He shrugged and took her arm briefly to start down the trail Carl and Mancho had followed. "I didn't get every word," he admitted, "but he seemed convinced that Mancho had broken loose. He didn't go into the cottage right away. He heard the shooting and thought it was at the target practice range so he went there. When he came back to the cottage it was empty, and the leg of the table to which Mancho had been chained was splintered. So I suppose Mancho could have broken it at sight of a couple of strangers."

"Or someone could have splintered the table leg to make it look that way," Anise replied, not at all convinced. "I'm sure I saw a shadow move across the window."

He frowned. "A breeze ruffling the curtain, perhaps. But I'll keep checking."

The approach to this beach was a gradual slant. At the edge of the sandy cove there was a bench where they could sit and watch Carl play with his dog. The boy threw driftwood sticks into the mild surf, and Mancho went bounding after them, coming back to shake so vigorously he gave Carl a shower. Sometimes, not waiting for a stick, Mancho bounded through the waves to leap for a bird diving for its breakfast. He and

Carl both chased any flock of gulls or other seabirds that landed in search of food.

"I think I should explain a little more of the situation here," Gregory said. "I want Bonnie to learn to love this place, and eventually to take care of it. When she's old enough, I'll start teaching her my lumber interests, too. I can see no reason why an intelligent woman couldn't handle such things as well as a man, if she is trained so well it becomes a natural part of her life. At this point I don't expect a male heir, so it will most likely all fall to Bonnie."

"All!" she exclaimed. "You mean—"

"I mean that except for a few bequests, she will be my sole heir. Or maybe I should say heiress."

She stared at him, amazed. "What about Laura?"

"Oh, she'll be taken care of, naturally."

"But not—not—I should think your will would divide the estate equally between your two daughters!"

His mouth was tight. "That's not advisable. The estate goes to Bonnie."

"But—but *why*?" No wonder Mr. Morton thought Bonnie was in danger! If someone here didn't want her to inherit this wealth of land and lumber . . . .

"I have my reasons." His voice had roughened and the brooding darkness was back in his eyes as he went on grimly. "One reason is that Laura is too completely under the domination of Melanie's family. Melanie hasn't been much of a mother, mostly because of her illness. But even in her lucid periods—"

He turned to her sharply. "How much do you know about the family situation here? Has Clay said anything?"

Remembering that Clay had been afraid he'd said too much, she replied quickly, "Clay told me you don't like for him to discuss your affairs, so—"

His brows lifted inquiringly. "Then you don't know that Bart Graham is Melanie's brother?"

"Well, yes, he did say that."

"And the Mortons are their cousins? Not first cousins—rather a shirttail relationship—but they've been a big help. I don't know how I would have managed if they hadn't taken care of Laura while Melanie was in a mental hospital. I wish I could say I trust them and Bart completely, but several things have happened—"

63

He was silent for some time, staring down at his hands clasped between his knees. Finally he sat up straight and gave her a rather bleak smile. "That's why I want you here with Bonnie. You can help me protect her interests."

She felt her face tighten. "Her interests, or her life?"

"Oh, it won't come to that! I'm not exactly broadcasting the terms of my will. Clay and I inherited this land from our father and—"

"Oh, then Clay owns half!" Somehow she hadn't gotten that impression.

"Not anymore." His face was grim again. "Clay was rather like the prodigal son in the Bible. He wanted his half of the inheritance in cash so he could tie into something more to his liking than timber and milling. Maybe he didn't squander his substance in riotous living like the man in the Bible, but he always enjoyed a good time, and had a lot of fair-weather friends. Besides, he was careless with his investments and finally went bankrupt."

Anise waited for him to go on. When he just sat there scowling at the sea, his hands again clasped between his knees, she said, "So he decided that lumbering wasn't so bad after all, and came to you for a job?"

He sighed deeply and smiled at her. "That's about the gist of it, simply put. And he's been quite a help. As a boy, he avoided the mill. Now he's taking hold competently. Unless there are labor troubles, or machinery breakdowns, or something like that, I can leave everything in his hands for weeks at a time. He likes children, too. I think you'll find him a help with Bonnie."

She nodded, remembering how kind he had been. "Then since Clay has already received his inheritance, I suppose he doesn't figure in your will at all."

He didn't answer for a moment, and she realized that it wasn't any of her business. She shouldn't have asked.

"Not prominently," Gregory said. "There probably wouldn't be much point, anyway. He'll most likely die first, the reckless way he lives. He's a bit too daring when it comes to flying, skin diving, and almost any kind of racing."

They looked up as Carl and Mancho came trudging across the dry sand, the dog still shaking water from his spotted body. As they passed near, Carl forced his gutteral voice to a

64

shout and called out something that sounded like, "Going home now!"

"Why does he live alone in that cottage?" Anise asked wonderingly. "I should think it would be simpler to have him in the house with the rest of us. It's so big there must be plenty of room."

"It isn't a question of room." Gregory's tone was hard again, almost bitter. "Melanie simply can't abide the sight of him. His mongoloid appearance is repulsive to her, and she possesses no sympathy or compassion. It's a mark of her type of mental illness—or any type, maybe—that she is concerned only with herself and the unreal world she lives in. Carl doesn't look normal to her, so she's afraid of him. And she's deathly afraid of the dog. Mancho shows an almost uncontrollable hostility toward her, too. He probably senses her fear and revulsion."

Anise gazed at him in rising uneasiness. "Then isn't it dangerous to have the dog around here at all?"

He shrugged, still looking unhappy. "I can't deny that poor boy his dog! They're practically inseparable, and he has no other companion. They do all right in the cottage with Deirdre and their mother to do the housekeeping. Melanie is never allowed outside except with someone who can control the dog. Any of us could except Miss Enid, but she has nothing to do with Melanie. She's here only to tutor Laura. And Bonnie too, eventually."

"Bonnie?" He had mentioned that before, she remembered as disappointment constricted her throat. "Then I suppose you won't need me after—"

"I'll need you all summer. Maybe longer. We'll see. That's about enough of the situation for you to absorb now, so let's walk back to the house. Miss Enid may have brought the children home from their little excursion. She took lunch for them, but it usually turns into a midmorning snack. Laura's a much bigger eater than Bonnie. She'll probably have a weight problem someday."

CHAPTER 7

Resting in her room, Anise reviewed the experiences of the morning, the things Gregory had told her. In retrospect they took on a menacing aspect she hadn't felt at the time. Who among her associates here could she and Bonnie trust? There was much suspicion evident among themselves, and she felt rising uneasiness over each one she considered. Even Gregory.

On the face of it, he seemed to be a father anxious for the best interests of his little daughter. But there was an underlying sense of hostility in his attitude, as if he might be using Bonnie for some vengeful purpose. And why disinherit Laura in Bonnie's favor? He had known and loved that daughter all her life, and certainly her poor, afflicted mother seemed more dear to him than Sylvia. He blamed his partiality on fear of family influence on Laura. Yet he showed more hostility toward the Dimmicks than toward the Mortons and Bart. It just didn't add up.

She wasn't accustomed to so much exercise, and her walk in the crisp sea air left her drowsy as well as weary. She was almost asleep when the bell rang for lunch.

She brushed her hair to bring out the blonde highlights, gave her makeup a little retouching, she asked herself derisively whom she was trying to impress.

could no longer rest, for anxiety about Bonnie had become a gnawing pain. The child had been so reluctant to leave her; she had looked so small and vulnerable following Miss Enid and Laura along that path so near the edge of the cliff. Then there had been that odd communication, almost a silent battle between Laura and her governess, as if they shared something hostile, or dangerous, but were not in agreement.

Hearing voices down the hall, she opened her door, hoping the picnickers had returned. No one was in sight, so she went to the head of the stairs, arriving just as Gregory and the Mortons descended them and crossed the entrance hall. They were all talking at once, so argumentatively she couldn't understand what they were saying. Before she could catch up with them they had gone into the living room, partially closing the door.

She stood uncertainly at the foot of the stairs, wondering whether or not to go in and join them. She would like to interrupt their argument long enough to ask about Bonnie. It was now after two o'clock, and Miss Enid apparently hadn't yet brought the children home.

Before she could make a decision, Miss Enid came running in the front door, so out of breath she could hardly speak. Her bone-thin face was white and beads of perspiration glistened across her forehead. Panic sharpened her pale gray eyes.

"Miss Weston, you'd better come—" she panted, her hand at her throat. "Bonnie's in the water—and I can't—" The words choked off on a gasp as she whirled about and ran out the door, down the path through the garden.

Anise was right after her, shaking with fear. Why on earth had Bonnie been allowed in the water? Everyone knew it wasn't safe! And as far as she knew, Bonnie couldn't swim!

She caught up with Miss Enid at the gate. They both stopped short as Gregory called out from the door. His long strides soon brought him beside them.

"What happened?" He looked angry. "What are you women so upset about?"

"Bonnie's in the water!" Anise cried accusingly.

The words must have acted like adrenalin in his blood, Anise thought, as he sprinted swiftly to the edge of the cliff and disappeared down the stairs. She tried to follow, but Miss Enid grabbed her arm in a painful grip, holding her back.

"Wait! Please!" Enid cried. "Don't tell anyone I panicked and called you. Maybe she was all right. I mean, they could handle it. There's nothing you could do, anyway. But I got scared—I didn't want you to blame me if—"

"I'm glad you warned us." Anise tried to free her arm from the clawlike fingers. "I've been worried for hours!"

"Then you won't tell anyone? I mean, Mr. Gregory knows, but don't tell anyone else I came for you. Please! They've got it in for me already, and this— They'll tease me to death!"

"Okay, okay!" Anise agreed, wrenching free. Her arm felt bruised from the woman's pinching fingers. She rushed to the top of the stairs and glanced about.

Gregory was running across the beach, lifting his feet high from the clinging sand as he shouted at Bart and Laura. They seemed to be playing in the surf, fully dressed. They were stooping over, their backs to the beach, their drenched clothes clinging to their bodies as the backwash of a breaker surged past.

But where was Bonnie? Anise felt her heart plunging downward faster than her feet could carry her down the stairs. Then the thick dry sand held her back, making it seem like trying to run in a nightmare.

When Bart and Laura could hear Greg's shouting above the roar of the surf, they turned, saw him, and yelled something back. Just then a breaker crashed over them both, burying them in foam.

"Where's Bonnie?" Anise quavered, weak with fear and effort as her straining legs brought her onto the smooth wet sand where she could walk more easily. Greg was already wading out into the churning water. When the submerged bodies came into view as the wave receded, Bart had Bonnie in his arms.

"Oh, thank God!" Anise murmured, pressing a hand to her chest to quiet the painful throbbing of her heart. But she was struck with new fear as she saw how limp Bonnie lay in Bart's arms.

Gregory strode into the backwash to take Bonnie himself. He upended her, holding her by her legs. She promptly began struggling and strangling as she vomited seawater.

Laying her on the hard-packed sand, face down, Gregory spread his big hands about her small rib cage and systematically pressed and released until Bonnie began to breathe normally. She immediately started wailing, her voice thin and hoarse.

Everyone had been talking at once, but, in her anxiety over Bonnie, Anise hadn't listened to their words. Apparently Greg hadn't either, for now as he picked Bonnie up in his arms, he glared around the group and asked sternly, "How did this happen? You've all been told to stay out of the water!"

"We were only wading," Laura whimpered, her shadowy green eyes bright with tears. Or was that only seawater?

"We only meant to let the waves chase us," Laura went on as Gregory turned his stern gaze on her. "I told Bonnie not to really go out in the water!"

"I told her so, too!" Miss Enid declared. "But she ran out there anyway and fell into one of those holes."

"We couldn't catch her!" Laura chimed in, more stoutly now that Enid was backing her up. "Then a great big wave came along, and—and she was gone."

"Lucky I was out surf fishing," Bart said. "You vetoed diving for abalone, so I told Fannie I'd see what I could catch from the rocks. I was out on the promontory when I saw the kids start to wade. I figured it was too dangerous, so I started in to warn them. That ledge hid them from my view part of the way, and when I got here they said Bonnie had been washed out. I thought I saw her head bob up once, so I dived in to look for her. But I couldn't find her until that last wave washed her in closer."

Gregory nodded and turned to Miss Enid. "Another such incident and you'll be sent packing! You should never have let them go near a surf like this!"

"I know! I warned them!" Her homely face was screwed up as if she were about to cry. "I forbade them! But you know how Laura is, determined to have her own way. Bonnie's starting out to be just as bad. They wouldn't listen to me. I could handle one, maybe—but they went in different directions!"

Bonnie was beginning to struggle in Gregory's arms, so he put her down. She ran straight to Anise.

"Somebody grabbed me!" she sobbed. "Somebody grabbed me and pulled me under!"

"Nobody grabbed her!" Miss Enid said sharply. "No one was anywhere near her!"

Gregory turned to Bart. "What do you think?"

Bart shrugged. "I told you I didn't see her go under. But you know what a pull the undertow has in a tide like this. It could make her feel that someone was pulling her under."

Was Bart telling the truth? Anise wondered. Or had he been right there with the others, seizing his first opportunity to drown Bonnie? Remembering how it had looked as she came running down the stairs, Anise had a suspicion that Bart could have been holding Bonnie underwater until Gregory's shout just before the breaker engulfed them.

Gregory was nodding, as if agreeing with Bart about the undertow.

"The thing is," Bart went on more confidently, "the kid doesn't know how to swim, so, the minute she stepped out into a hole and went under, she panicked. If she could swim, she would simply have held her breath until she could surface and coast in on the wave. Panic causes more drowning than anything. A swimmer is used to being underwater, and knows how to handle himself without panicking."

"You're right about that," Gregory agreed. The sternness melted from his expression as he gazed down at Bonnie and smiled. "I should have installed a swimming pool before you came, so we could give you swimming lessons. But we'll find quiet water in a lake soon, and I'll start teaching you. I want you to learn to feel at home in the water, then you'll be safer. Let's go to the house now and get dry clothes on."

He picked her up and set her on his shoulders, steadying her with his hands at her tiny waist. She clung to his thick, dark hair, looking uneasy on her perch as he strode across the dry sand to the stairs.

Following more slowly with Miss Enid, Anise said, "I appreciate your coming to warn us, Miss—"

"Sh!" Miss Enid flushed red to the roots of her short, neutral-colored hair and glanced about fearfully, as if afraid they were being overheard. But Bart had strode off toward the rocks, apparently to go on with his fishing. Laura was trudging ahead, her stocky legs almost able to keep up with Gregory.

"It wasn't necessary after all, as long as Bart came in time," Enid said. "Please—you promised not to say anything about the way I panicked."

"Well, okay, but I don't see why not. It was perfectly natural for you to—"

"No it wasn't! It made me look like a silly old maid—as if I didn't trust Bart. I got scared before they were really in danger, mostly because they wouldn't mind me."

Anise didn't know whether to believe her or not. Nothing seemed to add up right. She was glad she had written that letter to the Dimmicks. Before mailing it, she would add something about this episode, too, expressing her uneasiness, her doubts that Bonnie's near-drowning was only an accident. Perhaps with this letter, and a good lawyer, the Dimmicks could start building a case to win Bonnie's custody. Surely this wasn't a safe place for her!

Again the thought occurred to her that, with the letter written, where would she mail it? There were no corner mail boxes, apparently no RFD delivery and pickup, the nearest post office was no telling how many miles away. She would simply have to trust someone here to mail it for her. Who was most trustworthy?

She had the bleak feeling that the Dimmicks might never receive any letter she wrote. But if things got too bad, perhaps she could manage to use the phone.

Or could she? With a helpless sense of suffocation, she realized that she and Bonnie were virtual prisoners.

CHAPTER 8

In the entrance hall Gregory sent Laura to her room to change into dry clothes, telling Miss Enid to go help the child. Taking Bonnie down from his shoulders, he kept her in his arms as he stood back for Anise to precede him up the stairs.

"I'm sorry that Bonnie had this scare," he said, close behind. "I think Bart is right about the importance of her learning to swim before she develops any greater fear of water. There's a quiet lake not far from here. We'll fly over there as soon as I can find time, and I'll start giving her lessons."

He put Bonnie down in her own room, and turned to the hearth where a fire had been laid. "The poor kid's teeth are chattering," he said. "Better give her a hot bath to wash off the salt water and warm her little bones."

"I will," Anise agreed. She unzipped the brine-soaked dress. "Then she had better have a nap."

Gregory went into the bathroom to turn on the water. When Anise brought Bonnie in, wrapped in a robe, she noticed the sand clinging to his wet slacks.

"You'd better get into dry things yourself, Mr. Lockwood," she said, "before you catch pneumonia."

He turned off the water and grinned at her. "I'm practically immune to illness, Anise, look, you don't have to be so formal with me. Why don't you call me Greg, like everyone else?"

"Everyone else?" she challenged. "Miss Enid and the Mortons call you Mr. Gregory."

"That's different." His dark eyes were somber, his face unsmiling as he laid his hand briefly on her shoulder and said, "I'd like for us to be friends, Anise. I want you to trust me completely."

Before she could answer over the sudden pounding of her heart, his expression became casual again and he backed out of the room saying, "I'd better get the heck out of here so you can give Bonnie her bath."

After Bonnie was tucked into bed for her nap, Anise went to her own room and finished her letter to the Dimmicks, telling them about Bonnie's near drowning. She had the letter sealed and stamped when Gregory knocked on her door.

"How is Bonnie by now?" he asked. He was wearing taupe slacks and a luxurious looking sport jacket. The somberness was in his eyes again, reminding her of the way he had said he wanted them to be friends, he wanted her complete trust.

"I—I think she's asleep." Anise was disturbed to find her voice shaky. She cleared her throat and added more firmly, "She seemed drowsy after her bath."

He nodded and came on into the room. "I know you're upset about this incident, Anise, and I don't blame you. But I'm sure it was just an accident, and won't happen again. I've been talking very sternly to Laura and Enid. They have promised that the children will never again go into the water—not even to wade up to their ankles, unless Clay or Bart or I am there to guard them. It seems safe enough in shallow water, but one big wave can change the depth radically. Has Bonnie said anything more about her version of the accident?"

Anise shook her head. "I didn't want to bother her with questions. I'll talk to her about it later."

He nodded and was about to leave the room when she remembered the letter.

"Mr. Lockwood—Greg—how does mail go out of here? I've written a letter." She picked it up.

"Give it to me. Bart's driving the truck down to the cape to pick up a few supplies. He can mail it there." Taking it from her, he glanced at the address. A scowl darkened his face briefly, then his eyebrows lifted and he gave her a tight smile.

"I hope you're giving Bonnie's grandparents a good report

75

of her new home? And a better impression of her father, too. They believed Sylvia when she turned against me. Only natural, I suppose." He shrugged and shoved the letter into his pocket. "But I hope you will reassure them about my fitness to be her father."

Anise was glad he left before she had to answer. She stared at the door he had closed quietly, and felt a sense of guilt—almost betrayal—as she remembered how much fear she had expressed about this place and the danger it posed for Bonnie's life.

But maybe it's all true, she told herself. If there were a real threat to Bonnie here, she wanted the Dimmicks to know, so they could take steps to get her custody.

Yet what if it weren't true? What if the frightening things that happened were purely accidental, and Greg turned out to be as kind and concerned a father as he seemed at times?

Before she had thought further on the subject, Bonnie called out. Anise hurried to the child's room to find her sitting up in bed, her damp brown hair in tumbled disarray, her brown eyes huge with worry.

"I'm still scared," she whispered. "I can't go to sleep."

"I'm sorry, Bonnie. Would you like to sit in my lap a while?"

Bonnie promptly slid out of bed and followed Anise to the slipper chair by the window, cuddling up in her arms.

"Now tell me about it. I know it was terrible, being pulled under the water, whether it was the undertow or— Who do you think it was?"

Bonnie began to shiver. "I don't know—I just know something pulled me and there was water in my nose and I couldn't breathe! Let's go away from here, Miss Weston! I don't want to stay any longer."

"You'd have to live with your grandparents, Bonnie," Anise reminded her.

"I don't care. That's better than being here with that—that —I don't like Miss Enid. She told a lie. She didn't try to make us stay out of the water. She hardly paid any attention to us all day."

"All day? You mean not at the picnic either?"

Bonnie shook her head. "It wasn't a very good picnic. We just went to a little old park and played on swings and things.

76

out being attacked. I've begged him to either send them away, or let me leave. But he won't do it. Do you know why?"

Anise could only shake her head again, but her uneasiness was growing, for she began to doubt that Melanie was completely rational after all. Those green shadowed eyes, so much like Laura's, were taking on an unnatural glitter, and her pretty mouth was twisted out of shape.

"He thinks I don't suspect it, but I know what he's up to!" Her voice lowered to a conspiratorial tone. "He thinks if he keeps me frightened like this long enough, I'll lose my mind! He's trying to drive me crazy so he won't have to—to—"

She faltered and seemed confused for a moment. Then she went on with new fervor, talking faster, her voice rising, "He didn't really want to marry me, you know. I guess I had that figured all along, but I didn't realize. . . . It's dangerous here for you, too! Haven't you found that out by now? There are dark, vicious forces. . . . Oh, you can't imagine the gruesome things that go on! You should leave while you can! Take that child and get out of here—tomorrow may be too late! You've got to—"

She broke off as the door opened and Laura sidled in, glancing down the hall behind her before shutting the door, as if to make sure she wasn't being followed. She wore a pink wool robe, apparently having been taking a nap. Her taffy blonde hair had been brushed almost dry and hung loose about her shoulders.

"I heard you in here," she said, sounding breathless as she moved farther into the room. "I heard your voice and sneaked away from Miss Enid. Everybody tries to keep me away from you, Mother, and I've been wanting to see you!"

She ran a few steps and flung herself on Melanie, arms reaching up to hug her. But to Anise's amazement, Melanie's face twisted with an expression of revulsion—or maybe it was fear. She thrust the child violently away.

"Get out of here, you sprite! I told you never to follow me! What are you trying to do, anyway?"

Anise had found it difficult not to dislike the child. Now she felt genuine compassion as the little girl backed away, pudgy shoulders slumping, her face tight with threatened weeping, obviously distressed over the rebuff. She moved close to Anise, tears spilling over.

Anise held the plump little figure in the circle of her arm, and felt the child pressing close, seeking comfort. A moment later Laura wrenched away and stood defiantly before her mother, shouting, "All right for you! I'll tell Daddy how mean you are! Anyway, you haven't got all your marbles! I don't care what you say!"

She stuck out her tongue, whirled swiftly, and ran from the room, slamming the door behind her.

"They've got to get her out of here!" Melanie cried, getting to her feet in obvious agitation. "She keeps saying she's my child—keeps calling me Mother—but she's an ugly phoney—a bogey! She isn't real at all. I have no child! Greg's just using this—this monstrosity—to drive me crazy . . . so he can get rid of me and. . . ."

The woman lapsed into incoherence as she paced the room, wringing her hands. Anise knew her rational spell—if indeed she had been rational at all—was over.

Knowing she had better call for help, Anise headed for the door just as she heard Greg's voice somewhere down the hall. He was speaking angrily to someone, but Anise couldn't understand what he was saying.

Before she could get her hand on the knob, the door was thrust open and Mrs. Morton came rushing in, her face taut, her glance sharpening at sight of Melanie.

"How on earth did you get out?" she cried, pushing past Anise to cross the room. Melanie cringed as the woman took rough hold of her arm and poured out a torrent of vituperation.

The next moment Laura was in the room, followed by Greg whose presence immediately dominated the group as he took stern command.

"You may go," he told Mrs. Morton, encircling Melanie with a gentle arm. Melanie clung to him, trembling and whimpering.

Mrs. Morton released Melanie's arm, but met Greg's hard gaze with defiance. "Don't you think I can handle her? If I'm not giving satisfactory service—"

"I'm not accusing you of anything, Fannie. I simply want to take care of Melanie now. I'm sure you have plenty to do elsewhere. See that Laura goes back to her room, for one thing, and tell Miss Enid to keep her there."

She returned his gaze for another moment, then, tight-lipped and scowling, she left the room.

"I'm sorry this had to be your introduction to my wife," Greg told Anise, his dark eyes troubled as he gazed at her over Melanie's blonde head. I had planned to get you together in a pleasanter way as soon as Melanie was feeling better. She hasn't been well, you know."

"I know," Anise murmured, then watched in wonder at the tenderness Greg showed as he gently led Melanie out of the room and quietly closed the door.

Melanie had accused him of trying to drive her crazy, yet he had shown far more kindness and sympathy than Mrs. Morton, who was her cousin. And Melanie had clung to him as if she trusted him implicitly.

What a sad burden it would be to have a wife like Melanie, Anise thought, stricken with compassion. No wonder he had those dark somber moods of brooding melancholy. And with the heavy responsibilities he carried for this household and all his business interests, no wonder he seemed domineering at times. He had to be!

As admiration for him began to quicken her heart, she gave herself a stern warning. There were times, especially in his lighter moods, when he seemed so vital, so virile, he had stirred her deepest emotions. She must never let herself fall in love with him. It could mean nothing but heartbreak, since he was already married, and obviously devoted to his unfortunate wife.

She wondered how long Melanie had been insane. Why didn't he leave her in a mental hospital, instead of trying to take care of her in a place like this? Wouldn't it be better for everyone concerned, including Melanie?

While Anise was pondering the subject, Deirdre knocked on the door and came in. Her face was red, her eyes puffy as if she had been weeping.

"I'm sorry about Melanie coming in here to bother you," she said morosely. "I was supposed to be watching her. I did watch her! I had my eye on her every minute until she tricked me. She may be crazy, but she's plenty smart when it comes to tricking somebody!"

"I guess that's true of lots of mental patients," Anise agreed. "When she first came in here she seemed quite normal."

Deirdre nodded and blew her nose. "Mr. Greg said she should have a walk in the garden while Bart took Carl and his dog along in his truck to go after supplies. So Mom told me to go walking with Melanie and keep a sharp eye on her. We picked a bunch of flowers and brought them in to the sink on the porch. Melanie wanted her cloisonné vase, and she promised to stay right there while I went to get it." She drew a long, shuddering sigh.

"I can guess what happened," Anise said. "She slipped away while you were gone."

Deirdre sighed again. "I might've known. She's been curious about you and Bonnie all along. But Mr. Greg wanted her to start acting more sensible before he let her join the family and play hostess. Now she'll be off her rocker worse than ever, I suppose, and they'll all be down on me about it."

"It wasn't altogether your fault!" Anise declared. "Mental patients are completely unpredictable. I would hate to be responsible for her care!"

"You and me both," Deirdre agreed. "That's one thing I don't like about my job here. The work's okay. I'm not lazy. And Mr. Greg's not hard to work for if you do just what he says, but he sure scares me when I—if I make mistakes. Lots of times I'd leave in a minute if it wasn't for Mr. Clay."

"Clay?" Anise noted in growing wonder how the girl's expression changed. Her eyes blinked and brightened, a tender smile touched her lips, and her breathing quickened with an air of excitement.

"Don't you think he's wonderful?" she asked rapturously. "So much kinder and more polite than Mr. Greg. I bet he could do a better job of running the mill and lumbering, too. Sometimes he tells me how. . . ." She paused, sudden concern darkening her eyes. "I shouldn't say anything about that. He tells me secrets, but he wouldn't want me to pass them along."

"Then you must be very good friends," Anise suggested.

Deirdre nodded, her eyes bright again. "I guess I wouldn't even have my job if it wasn't for Mr. Clay. But that isn't the only reason I liked him. He's so good-looking, don't you think? Not sharp-faced like Mr. Greg. And out in the sunshine his light-brown hair looks almost gold." She gazed at the fog-blank window dreamily.

So Deirdre was in love with Clay, Anise thought with a pang of pity. Somehow she couldn't imagine that Clay ever would seriously return her fervor. Was he using her? Or simply the philandering type who made love to any woman who caught his fancy? She found her cheeks burning a little as she remembered the way his touch had affected her own pulse as he walked with her down to the beach. And he had thrilled her with an invitation to fly down to San Francisco and go dancing. Would he ever try to follow through? Had he ever taken Deirdre out on a date?

As if the question had been asked, Deirdre brought her dreamy gaze back from the window and smiled at Anise. "Don't tell anyone, but we went to a dance over at a lake once. He took me there in the airplane. It was wonderful. So romantic, flying up in the dark sky. He's a good dancer, too. Just about the best I ever danced with. But he didn't think my folks would approve, so we kept it a secret. You won't tell, will you?"

"No, of course not. I think it's fine for you to have a chance to get out and have some fun."

Deirdre drew another blissful sigh, then, as if coming back to earth with a jolt, she said, "Oh—the reason I came in—I mean, we wondered if you and Bonnie would like to have your dinner served up here, instead of your coming down to the dining room. The poor kid had such a scare. . . ."

"Yes, that would be nice," Anise said gratefully, glad not to have to dress up and go down to dinner.

CHAPTER 9

Deirdre served their dinner on trays in Bonnie's room. Sitting in front of the brisk fire, eating thin-sliced baked ham and candied sweet potatoes, Bonnie perked up remarkably, becoming almost gay. Her brown hair, dry now, caught golden highlights from the flickering fire. Brushed back simply, in the Alice-in-Wonderland style she preferred, it curled about her shoulders. She looked almost like a happy little girl, her cheeks flushed with warmth, amber lights dancing in her brown eyes.

"When is my—my daddy going to teach me to swim?" she asked, sounding eager, yet at the same time a bit fearful.

"As soon as he has time to take us to a lake, Bonnie. Do you really want to go? You're not afraid of your daddy now?"

Bonnie's smile faded. The small delicate mouth turned downward again. "He hugged me, and he scolded Laura," she said. "He scolded Miss Enid, too. But he didn't scold me at all. I think he likes me best."

Remembering what Greg had told her about his will, Anise was inclined to think that might be true. But why? He'd had little chance to know Bonnie. This morning he had been very affectionate with Laura. His will apparently didn't reflect a dislike of Laura, only distrust of her mother's family.

"I expect he loves you very much," she told Bonnie, "And

I'm glad you're no longer afraid of him. If you want to learn to swim, I guess you're not afraid of water, either, in spite of your frightening experience."

Bonnie regarded her gravely. "The water scared me—it was horrible! But my daddy said if I learn to swim I won't be afraid. Mr. Bart said so too. Didn't you hear them? I want to know how to swim so I won't be afraid, and Laura can't call me a scaedy-cat."

"She called you that?"

Bonnie nodded. "She wasn't scared of the waves at all. She ran right into one with all her clothes on. When it knocked her down she just laughed. She dared me to try it. But when I did, something pulled me under." She shuddered at the memory.

"Even when you learn to swim," Anise reminded her, "you must never go in the ocean without a strong grown-up swimmer there too. Laura shouldn't either."

After Bonnie had been tucked into bed for the night, Anise began to feel restless. She tried reading one of the books Greg had thoughtfully provided, but at the moment no fiction could compare in excitement to the events at Mendolair.

Presently she heard a plane circling the house. That must be Clay returning, she thought with interest. A little later she heard the jeep approaching.

She put the book down and changed from her robe into a sweater and long burgundy skirt. It would be fun to go down and see Clay, talk to him for a while. He had been very friendly, and wasn't moody like his brother. In a way, he seemed the most normal, regardless of his secret flirtation with the housemaid. Or perhaps because of it, she added whimsically, giving herself an amused smile in the mirror. She retouched her makeup, brushed her hair to a loose wave, gave herself a final inspection, then wrinkled her nose as she wondered why she was primping. Was it the thought of seeing Clay that made her heart beat faster? Greg would be downstairs too, no doubt. But she had been seeing him occasionally all day. Besides, he was married.

As she walked slowly down the stairs she heard their voices in the living room. The conversation sounded lively, rather urgent, yet not argumentative. She paused at the door a moment before knocking. When the conversation ceased abruptly at

85

her knock, she pushed the door partway open and asked shyly, "May I come in? Or is this private?"

"Oh—Anise! By all means, come in!" It was Clay who rushed over to open the door wider and extend a cordial hand for hers. "I was hoping to see you tonight."

He was dressed almost as when she had first seen him: gray slacks and sweater, high boots, black shirt open at the throat. Seeing him beside Greg, she found less resemblance than she had visualized. His full lips and snub nose gave him a boyish appearance in contrast to Greg's lean, dark face and sharper features. Greg was frowning now, as if irked by the interruption.

"Clay has been telling me about a machinery breakdown at the mill," he said stiffly.

"Oh, then—I mean, I'm sorry . . . . If you have business to discuss, I'd better not stay." Feeling as if she had been rebuffed, she tried to back to the door, but Clay was firmly holding her hand.

"No, stay!" His hand tightened and his eyes were eager. "I haven't had a good look at you yet—and you look good enough to eat in that luscious thing you're wearing. Anyway, I've finished my report, and there's nothing we can do about the mill tonight. Sit down and we'll make it a party."

She glanced uneasily at Greg, relieved to see that a tight smile had erased the frown. "Of course, stay, Anise. I didn't mean for you to leave. What bothers me is that I'll have to go to the mill tomorrow, for no telling how long. I had hoped to take you and Bonnie over to the lake and start teaching her to swim. How is she now?"

They all sat down and she told him about Bonnie's growing interest in learning to swim. He nodded.

"That's good. I'm glad she's getting over her shyness with me, too. Eventually the impressions Sylvia and the Dimmicks have fostered will fade completely. You should have brought her down to dinner."

He spoke mildly, but again Anise had the feeling that she was being reprimanded. "I didn't think it wise, since she was so upset," she said defensively.

"You mustn't pamper her over these little upsets. She had enough special attention immediately after the accident. By the time she had been warmed with a bath and quieted with a nap, she should have been ready to join the family. Laura was with us, behaving quite normally, in spite of the cruel way her mother treated her. She says you were a witness to that."

Anise nodded, and Greg turned to Clay. "Melanie is now disclaiming Laura, pretending she never had a child. It's quite disconcerting, yet I hate to forbid Laura to see her mother at all."

"No, I wouldn't do that," Clay agreed. His eyes now had the same grave, hooded appearance as Greg's. "Would you like me to talk to Melanie?"

Greg shook his head. "It wouldn't help. You can't talk sense to a schizo. I may have to send her back to the hospital. But she hates it there, and it doesn't do her any good either."

His mouth tightened in a grimace as he glanced at Anise. "You might as well hear the rattling of the family skeletons. You're bound to learn about them eventually if you stay here long."

"I'll stay as long as Bonnie needs me," she promised.

"Good!" Clay exclaimed, beaming at her. "In my opinion that will be for a long time!"

"I'm not sure that's my opinion," Greg said. She glanced at him sharply and found his expression once again dark and somber, a frown accentuating the winglike slant of his eyebrows. "If you insist on pampering her, encouraging her to live apart from the family . . . I almost sent Deirdre up to insist on your bringing Bonnie down to dinner. But she said neither of you was dressed."

"I didn't suppose it was that important," she retorted, irked that he was making such an issue of it.

"Well, maybe not," he admitted with a shrug, "but the point is I don't want too much made of these little accidents. Perhaps Bonnie is accident prone, but she should get over that as she becomes more familiar with the place, and with us. What I dislike is her tendency toward a persecution complex, especially as far as Laura is concerned. Laura has been lonely here. I was hoping the children would be good friends. Laura's willing. She seemed quite upset this evening over Bonnie's hostility."

"Then she should be kinder and more considerate when they're together!" Anise snapped. "She shouldn't tease her, or call her a scaredy-cat and dare her to do something dangerous!"

She returned his stern gaze, ready to go on with this argument. But Clay interrupted mildly, "I'll talk to Laura about that. I know she's inclined to be a little daredevil, and she's not used to being with other children. They're both very young, with much to learn. I agree it's important for them to get along together. You'll be gone before she wakes up tomorrow, Greg, but I'll have a little chat with her about this."

Greg nodded and seemed to relax. "You can tell Enid, too, that I want Bonnie tutored every day, along with Laura, beginning tomorrow. She can prepare a report for me on her grade level."

He stood up and his voice was quietly matter-of-fact now as he continued speaking to Clay. "I suppose you checked the plane over and refueled when you flew in?"

"It's ready for warm-up and takeoff at a moment's notice. Flew in like a breeze. Hardly a wisp of fog all the way."

"Good. I might as well leave now, so I'll be on hand to get troubleshooters on the job first thing in the morning."

He turned to Anise. "Tell Bonnie she's to join Laura for lessons with Miss Enid right after breakfast. That will give you a few hours to yourself every morning, to do as you please. Good night." He nodded at them both and left.

Smiling broadly, Clay stood up and caught her hand to bring her to her feet. "Now with old sourpuss gone, we can have some fun. How about spinning a disc and dancing? Or would you rather walk on the beach? I saw a new moon a while ago."

"I—I think I'd rather dance," she decided, remembering how their last walk in the moonlight had affected her.

"I would too," he agreed, going over to switch on the low mahogany console and pull out the turntable. "I haven't forgotten that we're flying down to San Francisco to go dancing some night. But we'll have to wait until Greg isn't using the plane. What kind of a beat would you like? Hard rock, an old-fashioned waltz, or something in between?"

Before she could answer, he took a record from the rack and said, "Here's a good waltz album. Let's try it."

With his arm about her waist as they began moving to the music, she knew why he had decided to waltz. It was more intimate, more dreamily romantic than the modern dances. He danced with effortless grace, seeming not at all bothered by the fact that his boots were moving over carpet rather than smooth flooring.

During a pause at the end of the first number, he kept his

arm about her and smiled, his face just above hers. "You're pretty wonderful, Anise," he murmured. "Don't let Greg send you away."

The music began again, so she didn't have to answer. By the time another long number had ended, she began to feel uneasy about the intimate way he was holding her, caressing her cheek now and then with his own.

"I think I'd better go back upstairs," she said, trying to ease out of the circle of his arm.

"So soon?" His arm tightened, not letting her go.

"Yes, I— This has been fun, but I don't like to leave Bonnie too long."

He released her then and frowned. "Don't you remember what Greg said about pampering that child? She doesn't need a perpetual guardian. She's perfectly safe in her room."

"Maybe so, but she gets frightened. This is all strange to her, radically different from the sheltered life she lived with Sylvia. She should have time to get used to things. And to people."

He shrugged, but he was smiling now. "I suppose you're right. But don't carry that coddling too far or Greg will send you packing, and I would be devastated!"

He turned off the record player and walked with her to the foot of the stairs. There he caught her hand to his cheek for a brief moment and said softly, "Good night, Anise. Sweet dreams."

She could feel the quickened beat of her heart as she walked upstairs to her room. It wouldn't be hard to fall in love with a man like Clay Lockwood, she thought tremulously. Then, remembering that Deirdre adored him, and apparently without encouragement, she told herself not to be an idiot.

I'm here strictly to take care of Bonnie until she seems safe and happy, if that time ever comes. The Lockwood men don't interest me in the least!

Bonnie wasn't happy about it the next morning when Anise told her she was to have lessons with Laura and Miss Enid.

"I'd rather go to a regular school," she pouted. "Like I did at home."

"There's no regular school around here, Bonnie. I should think it would be more fun having lessons than just wandering about with nothing to do. I expect Laura will be delighted to have someone else in class."

Bonnie wasn't convinced. She was still reluctant when Miss Enid got up from the breakfast table and said crisply that it was time for lessons.

"Come on, Bonnie," she added, as the child just sat there looking stubborn. "It will be nice having two children to teach now. Laura's looking forward to having a classmate."

Bonnie sighed and gave Anise a pleading glance. "Do I have to?" she asked, her brown eyes somber.

Anise nodded. "Yes, dear. Your daddy says you must. Go on, like a good girl."

Anise was sitting at her bedroom window just before noon, fascinated by the way the fog was lifting, like a gossamer shade being rolled up to reveal the row of pines and fir along the cliff. She heard the fast thumping of small feet in the hall, then the sound of Bonnie's door bursting open and banging shut.

Hurrying to Bonnie's room, she found the child hunched up on the bed, sobbing.

"Bonnie! What is it?" she cried, sitting on the bed to take the small trembling form in her arms. Bonnie clung to her and managed to swallow her sobs.

"I don't like going to class with Miss Enid. I'm scared!"

"Scared? What are you afraid of?"

"Miss Enid! The way she looks at me, like—like . . . . Oh, I don't know how to say it, but it scares me! And she's making me learn algebra! I didn't have to learn algebra in my school at home!"

Were they teaching algebra in the grades now? Anise wondered. She knew the curriculum had changed somewhat since she went to school.

"It won't hurt you to learn algebra, honey," she said mildly. "I bet you can learn it as well as Laura!"

Bonnie gazed up at her with worried brown eyes. "But Laura had a head start, and she makes fun of me when I don't know the answers. She calls me stupid!"

"That's not nice! If you haven't had enough math yet to understand algebra, Miss Enid should give you some extra lessons. I'll talk to her about it."

"Come to class with me," Bonnie begged. "Please! Then it won't be so scary. They won't be mean to me if you're there."

Greg wouldn't like it, Anise thought dismally. But she decided to go along anyway, find out what was frightening the child. Or was Bonnie's imagination working overtime, as Greg insisted? Was she developing a persecution complex?

The next morning when Miss Enid pushed back from the breakfast table, announcing it was time for lessons, Anise said casually, "I'd like to attend class today. Bonnie seems to be having trouble with math. Maybe if I hear the lesson I can help her."

"That would be a good idea," Miss Enid agreed cordially. "Laura's considerably more advanced because of her private tutoring, and it would be boring for her to have to spend too much time listening while I coach Bonnie. I'll give you the books and assignments, so you can help Bonnie catch up."

After several days of attending class, reviewing her own mathematics so she could help Bonnie, Anise wondered what on earth could have frightened Bonnie at her first lesson. Class was held in a large cheerful room adjoining the double suite Miss Enid shared with her pupil. Blackboards lined one wall, books another. Desks and tables were arranged to form a work or craft center in each spacious corner. There was a perfectly normal classroom atmosphere, and Miss Enid showed skill as a teacher. Except for math, Bonnie had no difficulty. She read as well as Laura, and worked on her social studies during the day so she could recite satisfactorily.

"You're not afraid of classes anymore, are you?" she asked Bonnie one evening.

"Not when you're there!" Bonnie replied quickly. "You'll keep on coming, won't you? It's different when you're there."

"What's different when I'm not there?"

Bonnie frowned, looking puzzled. "It's the way they fight without any words."

"Fight without words? Bonnie, that sounds ridiculous!"

"No it isn't! They look at each other like they're real mad, then they look at me, and it scares me." The child was so earnest that Anise couldn't accuse her of making it all up. But she was beginning to fear that Greg was right about the persecution complex. Or perhaps Sylvia had instilled so much fear and distrust in her that it would take a long time for her to feel at ease here.

Greg had returned from the mill after a couple of days, but was home for only one meal, seeming taciturn and distracted. Clay flew back to the mill with him for a few days, then they both returned. But again Greg was home only briefly before flying back. Clay didn't go with him this time.

"Greg's like a dog with a bone when something goes wrong at the mill," Clay said as they listened to the jeep grind its way off toward the hangar. "He can't think of anything else, just worries it constantly."

"I guess he has to," Bart said. They were still at the table, the adults sipping a last cup of coffee, while the children ate ice cream.

"Worrying doesn't do any good," Clay said lightly. "Things always work out eventually."

"Because he makes them!" Bart shot back. "He has a lot at stake in his lumbering business. I wish he'd give me a job there at the mill!"

"You have plenty to keep you busy here, if you do a good job of it," Clay said tartly. He turned to Anise. "Let's go out and watch Greg's takeoff."

No one else went along as she and Clay walked out to the garden. Before long they heard the engine of the airplane revving up. A few minutes later the small aircraft circled the house, its red and yellow lights blinking. Anise watched until the lights were lost among the stars in the northern sky. She pictured Greg sitting at the controls, his eyebrows pulled down over dark somber eyes, his mouth grim as it had been at dinner tonight when he spoke of possible sabotage of the mill machinery.

Clay had scoffed. "It's just wearing out," he had said. He took Anise by the hand now, playing with her fingers as he said, "Greg accused you of fostering a persecution complex in Bonnie. I'm afraid he's developing one himself. Every time something goes wrong at the mill, he hollers sabotage, sees crooks behind every saw and plane. I'm sure his men are all absolutely loyal."

"I—I'd better go back in," Anise said uneasily. The caressing way he was toying with her fingers sent little shivers up her arm. She wasn't sure she liked it.

"So soon?" Clay protested. "Look at that moon! It's almost full. I thought we might take a walk down to the beach."

"Not now. Bonnie should go to bed by the time I've read a couple of chapters of her book to her, supervised her bath and her devotions."

"Devotions? You mean you're teaching the kid to say her prayers?"

"Why not? It seems to help ease her fear of this place."

"You mean she's still afraid? Good lord, I'll have to take that child in hand! She should be getting used to us now. But of course, with Creg away so much. . . . He'll be able to spend more time with her after he quits worrying about the mill. Suppose you go put Bonnie to bed, then I'll show you how lovely our shore can be in the moonlight."

An hour or so later she was walking with Clay along the trail that bordered the cliff. The moon made a glittering silver path on the ocean, and outlined the rugged rocks of the promontory where the waves dashed into phosphorescent foam as they broke, then receded into onyx blackness.

"It's like a photographic study in black and silver," she said, excited by the beauty of the scene.

"This path leads to a small park farther along the cliff," he said. "It isn't far, but I guess we won't tackle it in the dark."

"I haven't been there," she admitted, "but Miss Enid took the children one day. Bonnie said Miss Enid had a rendezvous with a man in a car."

"What?" He turned to her with an amused laugh. "That old maid? I can't imagine a man even looking at her twice. Probably what happened was that she stopped some tourist about to trespass on Mendolair property. That little park is almost on our boundary line, and a public road gives access to it. There's a sign warning that it's private property from there on, but some people pay no attention to signs. I'll take you and Bonnie to the park someday, but for now I suppose we'd better head for the house."

At the promontory they paused again to enjoy the view. A layer of fog was rising out on the ocean, mist already dampening the salty air.

"We'll be socked in before morning," Clay said, "so it's a good thing Greg took off tonight. I'd better see if Bart's with Melanie. Sometimes she goes nuts with claustrophobia when the fog blows in. That's one reason why I don't think Greg should keep her here. But Greg doesn't care what I think."

"I've met Melanie now," Anise said as they turned toward the house.

"You have?" He caught her hand and stopped in the path.

93

"I didn't think she'd been lucid enough to make an appearance since you came. Did Greg introduce you?"

"Not the first time I saw her. We met in the hall." She told him about the encounter, amazed at how deeply it disturbed him.

"Have you seen her since?" he asked, remaining on the path, keeping a tight hold of her hand.

She told him about the afternoon Melanie had come to their rooms after Bonnie's near drowning.

He began to swear softly, half under his breath. "He's driving her wild! I swear, sometimes I think it's deliberate. He keeps her in this desolate place, too far from the psychiatrists who've tried to help her. And he lets Carl scare her with that vicious dog. He won't let me talk to her. You notice how quickly he refused when I suggested it the other night?"

"But why?" Anise asked sharply. She had never seen him upset before. His hand was trembling before he dropped hers and thrust his fists deep in his pockets.

"I'll tell you why," he said, sounding as if his teeth were clenched. "But for God's sake don't let Greg know I told you. Melanie and I were engaged once, before Greg ever entered the scene. When Greg tired of Sylvia, he started chasing Melanie and broke up our romance. He married her as soon as he could dump Sylvia. Then I guess he wished he hadn't, because he's been driving her crazy ever since. Insists on keeping her here and handling her emotional problems himself instead of—"

"I can't believe that!" she cried. It seemed completely out of character with Greg as she had come to know him lately.

"Wait till you know him better!" Clay warned her, taking her hand again. "Wait till he starts working on Bonnie, the way he did Laura, trying to turn her against me. The way he turned Melanie against me. I would take Melanie away from here and take good care of her, if only he would set her free. But he's like the proverbial dog in a manger. He doesn't really want her himself, but he'll go to any lengths to keep us from finding our love again. I stick around and do what I can to protect her and Laura. If it weren't for them, I'd never set foot on Mendolair or in Greg's precious mill!"

He was still so wrought up that his hand trembled, clinging to hers. She didn't quite know what to say, so she said nothing.

She could hardly believe all this about Greg, yet she had no reason to doubt Clay.

Abruptly his manner changed. He drew a long harsh breath, shook his head, and circled her shoulders with his arm to draw her gently against him.

"I'm sorry. I've frightened you, haven't I? You're shaking. Or are you cold?"

"I—I'm not cold." She placed her palms against his chest so he couldn't hold her quite so close. "It's just that—"

"I know. I shouldn't have told you all that stuff about the family, about Greg. And I guess I exaggerated a little about still wanting Melanie. Poor thing, I'm sorry for her. I would like to see that she has better care than she can have here with only Bart and the Mortons to look after her. But I'm not really in love with her now. Who could be in love with a ghost? That's all she seems to be anymore. A poor distracted ghost of the lovely girl she used to be."

As she continued to push away he said, "Don't be afraid of me, Anise." There was tenderness in his voice, gentleness in the arm circling her, so she relaxed and let him draw her closer.

"I'm not afraid of you, Clay," she murmured, "but I must go back to the house and take care of Bonnie."

"Okay, we will." He made no move, however, except to tuck his finger under her chin and tilt her face up to his. Her heart began to pound frantically as she realized he was going to kiss her, and she was afraid she was going to let him.

With his mouth an inch from hers, they were startled apart as a shot rang out, like that of a rifle. It split the night silence, blasted over the promontory, then went reverberating through the forest behind them.

Clay grabbed her hand and ran with her toward the shadows of a group of deodora trees. While they ran, another shot was heard.

"Quick! Keep down!" Clay snapped. "We were silhouetted up there like a pair of sitting ducks!"

"I heard a bullet whiz right past us," she said shakily.

"I did too. Someone must have been shooting from the promontory path. We can make our way back to the house through the trees."

"You didn't believe me that day I told you someone was

shooting at Bonnie and me. Now they're shooting at me again!"

"More likely at me!" Clay said, his arm about her now as they made their way cautiously toward the house, keeping in the darker shadows. "It would hardly be hunters out shooting around this time of night. Believe me, I'm going to do some investigating!"

Anise drew a sigh of relief when they reached the house. Inside the entrance hall, Miss Enid and Laura were talking together excitedly, sounding out of breath.

"Someone's shooting out there!" Miss Enid said, her neutral-colored eyes glittering like glass in the hallway lights, her pinched face looking longer than ever.

"I heard them too," Laura chimed in, wide-eyed.

Afraid that Bonnie was awake and frightened, Anise started up the stairs. She looked down as Mr. Morton came from the back hallway, followed by his wife.

"Some damn fool's out shooting in the dark," Mr. Morton said disgustedly. "I took a look, but I couldn't see anyone."

Anise started upstairs again but paused as the front door burst open and Bart rushed in. "I thought I saw someone running along the promontory," he said breathlessly. "I was afraid to stay out in the open while chasing him, and by the time I got through the woods, nobody was there. Melanie's scared silly. I'd better get back to her."

He ran up the stairs and dashed past Anise to disappear down the length of the hallway.

Anise hurried to Bonnie's room, relieved to find the child sound asleep. She wondered if she, herself, would be able to sleep at all this night.

CHAPTER 10

Lying in the dark, thinking about it, Anise found herself more frightened than she had been at the moment the shots rang out and a bullet whizzed past her ear. She had been startled at that time, but the full significance of the attack didn't press in on her then as it did now.

Who could have been shooting at them? Was she, or Clay the target? Or both? Somehow she had the shaky feeling that she was the one. But why?

Does someone think I'm protecting Bonnie too carefully? she wondered. Bonnie would be easier to dispose of without a constant guardian. She would be completely vulnerable to any evil plan to get her out of the way.

The urge to take Bonnie and escape from this place became so strong she couldn't sleep. She wondered if her letter had ever been mailed to the Dimmicks. When she had asked Bart about it the day after Greg took it, he had replied carelessly, "If it was in that batch of stuff Greg gave me to mail, I mailed it. But I never checked it over to see what was there."

Even if the Dimmicks acted on the alarming information she had sent them, they might be too late. She thought of phoning, but even then it would be some time before legal processes could take Bonnie away from here. Meanwhile, anything could happen!

I won't leave without Bonnie, no matter how often I'm shot at, she resolved. She longed to bundle her up and make their escape somehow. But she could be arrested for kidnapping if she took Bonnie away without authorization. Besides, how could she manage their transportation? They were prisoners here unless the Dimmicks came to their rescue.

She was still trying to think of something constructive when the air was rent by a blood-curdling scream somewhere outside. Immediately a wild commotion seemed to break out all over, men shouting, the dog barking.

Anise jumped out of bed and ran to the window, throwing it open to peer into the darkness. A couple of flashlights moved about, illuminating nothing.

The scream was repeated. It sounded like a woman, Anise thought. It sounded like Melanie. The barking grew wilder, the shouting louder, until a shot blasted her eardrums, seeming to erupt from right below her window, putting an abrupt end to all other sound for a long, sickening moment.

Anise could make nothing of the confusion that followed. She pulled on her robe and went into Bonnie's room. Bonnie was sitting up in bed, her face pale and eyes wide in the glow from the night lamp.

"I heard something," she whimpered. "Did somebody shoot Laura's mother?"

"I don't know what happened," Anise said, sitting on the bed to take the trembling child in her arms. "Whatever it was, probably had nothing to do with us. Why don't you lie down and try to go back to sleep? We'll find out all about it in the morning."

"Let's find out about it now! I'm scared."

"Okay, you wait here and I'll see if someone can tell me what happened."

She went out into the dimly lighted hall just as Deirdre came up the stairs wearing a limp quilted robe over dark red pajamas. Her hair was up on big rollers.

"I suppose that shot woke you up?" she asked, not sounding very perturbed.

"I wasn't asleep," Anise told her. "Was that Melanie I heard screaming?"

Deirdre nodded. "Yes, but everything's all right now. Somehow Melanie got out and was wandering around on the grounds by herself. Then someone let Mancho loose. I don't believe he would really attack her, but she's so scared of him it gets the dog all excited. Anyway, Carl got there before any harm was done."

"But there was shooting!" Anise still didn't feel assured.

"Oh, that. I think it was Dad, just notifying everyone that Melanie was found so the search was over." She chuckled. "Everyone was out hunting for her. She wasn't supposed to be out of the house. But this time. . . ." Deirdre's smug satisfaction was obvious as she repeated, "This time they couldn't blame me for her slipping away. I wasn't on duty."

It was a long time before Bonnie quieted down enough to go to sleep and still later before Anise finally dozed off. When she woke up, Deirdre was smiling down at her, looking fresh and pretty in a crisp white apron, her hair neatly brushed.

"You slept right through the breakfast bell," she said. "So did Bonnie. I knew you were disturbed in the night so I decided to let you sleep. If you want to get up now I'll serve your breakfast here. Everyone else has eaten."

The window was opaque with fog again, but breakfast was cheerful before a warm hearth fire. Afterward they went down the long hallway that had now become familiar, to join Laura and Miss Enid in the classroom. It was warm and pleasant there, too, with a fire in the grate. Laura was working a math problem on the blackboard.

"Sorry we're late," Anise apologized.

"That's quite all right," Miss Enid assured her genially. "I understand you were disturbed in the night. Being over in this wing, we didn't hear much of it. I've started Laura on a series of problems to work out. I have some simpler ones for Bonnie to try. I'd like to see her catch up with Laura as soon as possible so they can work together."

With both little girls absorbed in their problems, Miss Enid gestured for Anise to follow her to a door at one side of the room. It led through a narrow inner hallway into a meagerly furnished bedroom which was apparently where Miss Enid slept. It had little of the warmth and beauty that Greg had provided for Anise and Bonnie. Just a narrow bed, a matching highboy and vanity, a well-worn upholstered chair and a couple of small tables.

Miss Enid's manner immediately became conspiratorial. "I

feel I've got to warn you, Miss Weston," she said in a loud whisper, casting wary glances toward the door she had closed behind them. "It isn't safe for Bonnie here, or for you either. I've been hearing things. There's too much family here. They think Bonnie's a threat to Laura—to her sharing in their father's estate. Maybe it sounds crazy, but hasn't Bonnie got any relatives to take care of her? I think you should get her away from here as soon as—"

She broke off as the door was thrust open and Laura stood there pouting, her green eyes hard in her tight little face.

"What did you come in here for?" she demanded. "I need your help with these old problems. You didn't tell me how to—"

"All right, all right," Miss Enid replied nervously. "I'd like to show Miss Weston my room. If you'll just look at your book I'm sure you can work those problems by yourself."

"No I can't!" Laura's taffy braids swung out as she shook her head. "Why do you want to show her this crummy old room? Daddy pays you to teach me!"

"Yes, I know." As Miss Enid meekly followed Laura back to the classroom, Anise had the distinct impression that the woman was afraid of the child. Hadn't Bonnie said something to that effect once? But it seemed crazy.

As if reading her thoughts, Miss Enid turned back at the classroom door to whisper, "That little brat isn't above telling her dad a lot of ugly lies about me if she thinks she's not getting enough attention. This may not be the best job in the world, but I don't want to lose it."

The fog was dissolving into a pearly translucent mist by the time lessons were over.

"Let's go outside for a while before lunch," Bonnie suggested as they left the classroom. "It makes me feel sticky to stay in the house all the time."

Anise felt the same way, so they put on their sweaters and walked through the garden, past the reservoir, following the trail that Gregory had shown her; the safe path they were permitted to explore anytime they wished. Bonnie went skipping ahead as they walked through the woods, stopping now and then to listen to the chatter of birds that seemed to be flocking along in the treetops, keeping just ahead of them.

When they came out into the open meadow with its mean-

100

dering stream, they saw a man digging near the foot of the small rise that bordered the woods beyond.

"That's Mr. Morton," Bonnie said, stopping to stare at him. "Let's go over and see what he's planting."

Greg had said they should always remain on the trail, but it seemed safe enough to walk that far across the meadow, since it was in the opposite direction from the dangerous cliffs.

As they approached, Anise saw Mancho lying beside the oblong hole the man was digging. She gasped and caught Bonnie's arm. "There's the dog! Don't go any closer!"

As they paused, Mr. Morton looked up and saw them. "You needn't be afraid of Mancho anymore," he said, his voice harsh with some deep emotion. "He's dead."

"Dead!" Moving slowly closer, Anise saw that the big spotted dog was indeed dead. She realized, too, that it was a beautiful dog. She had been afraid of it, ready to agree with Melanie and others who thought such a vicious dog shouldn't be allowed on the place. Yet, seeing the once swift, powerful creature lying there lifeless, she felt a strange sense of loss.

"Who—who killed him?" Bonnie quavered.

"I did. I shot him last night." The man began digging again. He tossed a few shovelfuls of earth aside, then leaned on the shovel to glare at Anise and Bonnie.

"It's a mortal sin to kill a fine dog like that! He wouldn't have been cross if he hadn't been chained up. Some folks teased him too, to make him more vicious. But Carl could handle him, anytime!"

He bent to lift a few more shovelfuls of earth, then paused again. "I had to kill him, because somehow he had it in for Melanie, and she kept getting out. And someone kept letting the dog loose. Carl had him out on leash last night, and chained him up again when they got back to the cottage. But while they were out, someone must've loosened the stake, because it was dragging on the chain when Mancho tried to attack Melanie. Or anyway, he thought he did, but I don't believe it. Did you hear her screaming?"

"Yes, and I heard the shot."

The man's face crumpled as he squeezed his eyes shut. Anise was afraid he was going to cry. It must have hurt him terribly to kill his retarded son's pet.

"I had to shoot him," he said thickly, "before he hurt her,

101

or maybe even killed someone, and Carl got blamed. It wasn't Carl's fault!"

Suddenly he was glaring at her, then at Bonnie, before his hostile gaze returned to Anise. "We didn't have trouble like this before you came! I warned you that day I had to bring you here! I've warned Mr. Greg! It ain't safe for you, or for anyone else around here, the way things are now! I told Mr. Greg, and you can see now I was right!"

"But why?" Anise cried. "What have we got to do with all —with the crazy things that keep happening?"

His mouth tightened. "If you can't figure that out, then I can't help you. I don't know all the ins and outs of family affairs, I'm not supposed to know about the will or anything. I only know there's a lot of hate around here, and it's a hundred times worse since you and the kid got here! I wish Mr. Greg would send you both away, and I'm going to tell him so!"

"If he won't, why not take us to the airport yourself? Without telling anyone? We're anxious to leave!"

He began digging again, furiously tossing one shovelful after another. "You know I can't do that," he growled. "I only do what Mr. Gregory tells me to. That's why I've still got my job. It's more than just a job. He's taking care of—of a lot of things you don't know about."

Anise tried to question him further, but he refused to say any more.

"I said too much already," he snapped, not stopping his work. "Go on and take your walk. But for God's sake, be careful!"

Anise took Bonnie's hand as they walked back to the trail. "Shall we go on farther?" she asked. "There's another beach at the end of this trail."

Bonnie shook her head and shuddered. "I don't feel like walking anymore. Mr. Morton scared me. Let's just go back to the house."

"That suits me," Anise agreed. Yet as they approached the tall rambling structure with its cupolas and gingerbread, she wondered if they were any safer there than out in the open.

"Why don't we go away like Mr. Morton said?" Bonnie asked plaintively. "I don't think anybody wants us here. Let's go far, far away."

"Your daddy wants you here, honey. I think everything will be better when he comes home. Your Uncle Clay loves you,

102

too." She hoped she wouldn't have to tell the child they were virtually prisoners.

"I'm still scared," Bonnie insisted, her dark eyes worried as she gazed up at Anise and clung to her hand. Her face was pale in the hazy sunlight. Drops of moisture from the condensing fog sparkled on her brown hair. "If you'll come with me, I'd even rather live with my grandpa and grandma."

"I've written to them," Anise told her. "We may hear from them next time any mail is delivered. Or they might come here to take us away."

"Really?" Bonnie's face brightened. Anise was afraid she had raised false hopes. Yet, with her letter detailing the possible dangers, the ruggedness and isolation, it was possible that the Dimmicks could obtain a court order to release Bonnie from Greg's authority. Always providing, of course, that her letter was mailed.

If things got worse she would try to phone them. The difficulty with phoning was the lack of privacy. The only phone she knew of here was the one in the central hallway where she would be heard by anyone almost anywhere in the downstairs living area.

In a way she would hate to leave, Anise reflected as she gazed out over the ocean which was turning blue wherever full sunlight broke through. The woods, the beaches, the rugged coastline were all fascinating and beautiful. Even the old house had a charm of its own. The persons here, too—each individual was interesting in his own way. If only she could trust them! If only there weren't this sense of danger, this menace lurking in every incident, she felt they could both be happy here. Especially if Greg were here more of the time, and in his pleasanter moods.

As she thought of the Dimmicks coming with legal authority to take them away, she found herself hoping it wouldn't happen before Greg returned. Maybe by then the situation would have been resolved, with all danger past, so they wouldn't want to leave.

When the lunch bell rang, after they had rested briefly in their rooms, Anise found the walk had given her an appetite. Bonnie, too, seemed more interested in her food than usual. The conversation was carried on mostly by Clay and Bart who were discussing the difficulties Greg was having at the mill. Finally Clay turned to Anise and said, "This can't be very interesting to you!"

"Oh, but it is!" Anise assured him politely. "Will Greg be coming home pretty soon?"

Clay nodded. "When he phoned this morning he said things are going pretty well now. He'll wait to be sure before he leaves. I suggested that he bring Carl a new dog. A pup he can train to be more friendly than Mancho ever was."

"Then he'll be no good as a watchdog," Bart remarked.

"What of it?" Clay snapped. "With someone around here so quick on the trigger we shouldn't need a dog. I'd still like to know who took pot shots at Anise and me last night. I'm not at all sure any strangers were around. Morton swears he didn't, so if you—"

"Don't try to pin it on me!" Bart said angrily. "I told you I was up in Melanie's suite! If it wasn't Morton, it must have been some tourist or poacher around the place. That's why we need a watchdog!"

"We supposedly had a watchdog!" Clay retorted. "What was Mancho doing while poachers roamed the place?"

"He was probably chained up at the cottage where he couldn't detect an intruder down here."

As the men glared at each other, Laura said cheerfully, "I think it will be nice if Daddy brings a puppy. A cute little one. Not an old meanie like Mancho!"

Clay smiled at her. "Greg should bring you a toy poodle, and bring Carl a well-trained, year-old Doberman or German shepherd. I'll tell him next time he phones."

Laura agreed happily, then turned to Bonnie. "Want to come up to my room and play? I've got a new game I haven't shown you yet."

"You'd better wait awhile," Miss Enid told her. "You promised to finish the problems you skipped this morning."

Laura's round face flamed red. "I don't have to!" she said, thrusting her lower lip out as she faced her teacher. "My daddy says I don't have to do lessons in the afternoon!"

She turned back to Bonnie. "You can come and play with me. Right now."

Bonnie shook her head. "I don't want to. I'm going to stay with Miss Weston."

Tears gathered in Laura's eyes as she stared at Bonnie. "Nobody does anything I want anymore!" Thrusting her plate

104

across the table with force that knocked a tumbler of water over, she pushed back from the table and ran sobbing from the room.

"I'll call Deirdre to clean up the mess," Miss Enid said, sighing as she got up to follow her charge.

By the time Anise and Bonnie had read awhile and played a couple of games, Bonnie was restless again. "Let's go down to the beach," she suggested. "It looks sunny and warm outside now."

Bonnie was right, Anise realized as they walked down the cliff steps to the beach, not even needing a sweater for warmth. The sun was bright on a surf that looked safe enough for swimming until a large wave crested and broke into foam, warning her there was probably a strong undertow.

Crossing the sand, Anise saw a neoprene suited figure sitting on a rock at the edge on the cove. At first she thought it was Bart, but, approaching closer, she saw that it was Carl.

"Where's Bart?" she called out.

Carl jumped up, as if he had been lost in thought and her call startled him. He sat down and polished the lens of his mask, saying truculently, "Bart didn't come. I'm going alone."

"Oh, but you must never go in alone!" Anise protested. "It isn't safe!"

He gave her a look of disgust, the flat eyelids narrowing his eyes to dark slits, his mouth pulled down at the corners.

"I don't care if it isn't! Dad shot my dog!" He broke down for a moment and cried like a child.

"I'm sorry," she said, laying her hand on his sleeve. "I'm terribly sorry. But I think Greg is going to bring you a new dog. A puppy, maybe."

"Don't want a puppy!" Carl snatched his arm from her touch, and wiped his tears with the back of his hand. "I want Mancho!"

He put on his mask, then removed it to wipe the lens again. Pausing, he stared out over the water. When he spoke, his voice had its usual gutteral tone, yet the slow, relaxed way of pronouncing each word made it easier for her to understand him than ever before.

"It's pretty . . . way out there . . . way down deep," he said. His drooping figure and the lack of spirit in his voice gave him an air of utter discouragement and resignation as he went on slowly, "You only hear your breathing . . . and the bubbles. You only see fish and seaweed . . . and big rocks like castles. It's green and soft and nobody yells at you. . . . I'll go live there."

Anise caught a sharp breath. "You *can't* live there! You haven't even got a scuba tank on! You'll drown if you try to stay down more than a minute!"

"Don't care!" He put on his mask, adjusted his weighted belt, and started for the surf.

"No!" she cried, running after him. "You mustn't do that, Carl!" She grabbed his arm, but he shook loose and strode on. She caught up and grabbed him again, pleading desperately. He pushed her down and walked faster. She watched in horror as he waded into the surf and disappeared under a cresting breaker.

"He's going to kill himself," Anise sobbed as Bonnie came running to her. She scrambled to her feet and caught Bonnie's hand. "Hurry! We've got to find Bart or someone to go after him!"

They found no one in the front part of the house. Panting with effort and anxiety, Anise ran back to the kitchen where Mrs. Morton was doing something at the sink.

"Quick! Where's Bart or Clay—or anybody who can skin dive and find Carl!"

"What happened?" Mrs. Morton's hand flew to her throat. Her gaunt face went pale as Anise told her that Carl had gone diving alone. "With no tank—not even a snorkel! He's going to kill himself because his dog is dead!"

Mrs. Morton looked ready to faint as she dashed for the stairs. "George and Clay are up at the reservoir," she panted, "but Bart. . . ."

Anise and Bonnie followed as the woman headed for the schoolroom. Bart was there, apparently playing the game Laura had wanted Bonnie to share. He listened placidly while Mrs. Morton voiced her alarm.

"Don't worry," he scoffed. "That kid will come up for air soon as he gets a snootful of seawater. He's just trying to make everyone feel sorry for him. He probably wouldn't have gone out at all if no one was there to watch and send for a rescue team."

106

"You can't depend on that!" Mrs. Morton argued. "Carl feels a lot worse over losing that dog than anyone knows! Anyone but me! I know how he feels—like life isn't worth living! You go down there and bring him out of the surf, Bart Graham! I'm holding you responsible for his life! You're the one who taught him to skin dive!"

"Okay, okay," Bart said, grinning as he headed for the door. "But I bet we'll find him safe and dry on the beach!"

"You get on your diving suit just the same!" Mrs. Morton ordered, stalking after him. "My bet is you'll have to pull him out of the water."

As Anise and Bonnie started to follow, Miss Enid said, "You'd better leave Bonnie here with Laura, if you're going back to the beach. The children would be in the way down there, and maybe even in danger. Bonnie can take Bart's place and finish this game before Laura throws a fit."

It seemed a feasible suggestion, so Anise told Bonnie to remain. When she saw the child's reluctance, she repeated the order, adding, "I'll come right back and tell you all about it."

Mrs. Morton had rushed out of the house. Anise followed swiftly. When she caught up with the woman at the head of the cliff stairs, she found that Miss Enid had followed her.

"Shouldn't you stay with the children?" Anise asked sharply.

Miss Enid shook her head. "They'll be all right for a few minutes. I'm anxious to see if Bart can find that poor boy. I never liked him much, but I'm sorry for him."

Carl was nowhere in sight as they hurried down the rickety steps.

"He could be dead by now," Mrs. Morton moaned as they struggled through the thick dry sand. "Why doesn't Bart hurry! I suppose he'll take his own sweet time putting on his scuba gear. He wouldn't care if Carl did drown! But if he does, I'll see that Bart Graham never sets foot on Mendolair again!"

It seemed a frightfully long time before Bart came down the stairs in his neoprene suit, his tank strapped to his back. Mr. Morton was following close behind.

"I told you he was drowning himself!" Mrs. Morton scolded between sobs as she stood on the wet-packed sand, wringing her lean, gnarled hands. "I told you he was desperate!"

Bart didn't answer. He strode past her, waded into the surf, and dove through a breaker, disappearing from sight.

Mr. Morton came across the sand more slowly. He stood beside his wife and put an arm about her shoulders as he said in a choked voice, "Don't cry, Fannie. Bart will find the boy in time. I hope."

CHAPTER 11

The time seemed interminable as they stood waiting, trying to believe that Bart could find the boy in time.

The moment a black helmet surfaced out near the rocky end of the cove, Mr. Morton waded into the surf, battling the waves until Bart reached him. Together they dragged Carl's bulky, unconscious figure up to the hard-packed sand. Mr. Morton stripped off the helmet and upper part of Carl's suit. Bart began a rhythmic pressure to force water out of his lungs. In a little while Carl began to cough and sputter. That subsided, and he stopped breathing again. For a while the two men took turns applying mouth-to-mouth resuscitation, and finally Carl was sitting up, shaking his head, beginning to weep noisily.

"Let me go back!" he sobbed. "Let me stay there! I won't live without Mancho!"

"Snap out of it, Carl!" Bart sounded stern and angry. "If you act like this, Greg will send you back to school. Or to a worse place where they'll lock you up to keep you safe."

"No!" Carl sobbed all the harder.

Anise glanced up and saw Clay walking across the sand. "The children told me what happened," he said as he approached. "I have the jeep up there. We'd better take Carl back to the cottage and give him his sedative."

It took a strong man on each side to urge Carl on as he stumbled and dragged his feet in the sand. Anise started to hurry on ahead, uneasy about the children being alone at the house. Miss Enid caught her arm.

"Wait, Miss Weston. I've been wanting to talk to you, but Laura never gives me a chance. She's the most demanding child I've ever had charge of. Like the way I couldn't even get you off to my room for a minute without her butting in. Besides, Bonnie's always with you, and I've wanted to see you alone."

Anise paused to listen, gently extricating her arm from the woman's clawlike grasp. There was something rather frightening about the way Miss Enid's neutral-colored eyes glittered in her sharp, bone-thin face.

"Bonnie's such a sweet, shy child," Miss Enid went on, speaking fast and urgently. "I hate to see her harmed. Or you, either. But someone here is out to get you both, for some reason. I think the Mortons are behind it. They're kin to Melanie, you know, and, actually, they run this household. They want to keep on running it—but not for you and Bonnie."

"Why not? I mean they're not running it for us!"

"They're afraid they'll have to. I think Mr. Gregory has threatened to give you full authority, or something."

"That's crazy!" Anise exclaimed. But on second thought, was it? Bonnie was to inherit Mendolair and all the lumber interests, and, meanwhile, as soon as she was old enough, she would be trained to manage everything. If he wanted Anise to remain with Bonnie—to help her perhaps. . . .

She remembered his criticism, and smiled as she told Miss Enid, "I doubt if I'll ever have any more authority than I have right now. He thinks I pamper Bonnie too much."

"No more than she needs—in such danger here! Pampering won't hurt such a good child anyway. I wish Laura behaved as well."

Anise tried to walk on, but Miss Enid hung back, continuing to talk, her manner urgent, so it seemed rude to go off and leave her.

"Laura's better now than she was at first. I'm almost fond of the child and I'd hate to lose this job. It's easier than teaching a class in public school. I was afraid, at first, that Mr. Gregory sent for you to replace me, so if I was a bit, well, unfriendly I hope you'll excuse it."

"It's all right—think nothing of it," Anise said, again walking on.

"Wait!" Mis Enid urged. "I want you to know that, if you are put in charge, I'd lots rather work for you than for the Mortons! They seem to think they're in charge whenever Mr. Greg's gone."

"What about Clay? I thought he was in charge when—"

"Oh, he never enforces anything. He's all right, but I don't think Mr. Gregory gives him much authority. Treats him more like a kid brother who isn't very bright."

Anise frowned, pondering that. It wasn't the impression she had gleaned of the relationship. But Miss Enid had been here longer, so was probably more accurate in her judgment.

Still lagging back because of Miss Enid's irritating slowness, Anise noted that all the others had moved out of sight at the top of the cliff. She hurried to the stairs and started up. Miss Enid, panting behind her, again called for her to wait.

"We should get back to the children," Anise said. "I never feel easy about leaving Bonnie for long. You said yourself that it isn't safe." She waited impatiently at the top of the stairs.

"She'll be all right with Laura. Anyone wanting to harm her would know he couldn't get away with it. Laura's such a tattletale." Miss Enid persisted in her infuriatingly slow pace.

In spite of Miss Enid's assurances, Anise found her steps quickening to match her speeding pulse as she rushed down the hallway to the classroom door.

The room was empty and silent, the game pieces scattered as if the game had ended abruptly. They went through the narrow corridor to Miss Enid's room, then to Laura's room. There was no sign of the children.

"Maybe they've gone to our suite," Anise said, her flesh beginning to prickle with alarm.

They weren't in her room, nor in Bonnie's, nor could they be found anywhere in the house. Anise resisted the urge to say, "I told you there was danger!" as they searched the lower floors.

Hearing sounds upstairs, they went back up and found that Deirdre had come in the back way.

"Melanie's gone!" Deirdre cried, sounding frantic. "I left her locked in her room while I went to the cottage to build a fire and heat water to take care of Carl. They've taken Carl there now in the jeep, so I hurried back. And Melanie's door has been unlocked by someone. She's gone!"

"Have you seen the children?" Anise asked sharply.

Deirdre shook her head. "I—I thought they were with you. I was busy with Melanie until I went to the cottage. Nobody came to the cottage with Carl except my folks and Bart, and Mr. Clay."

"Maybe those children are with Melanie," Miss Enid said. "Laura grabs every chance she gets to be with her mother. We'd better find them quick! Phone the cottage, Deirdre, and tell Mr. Clay—or your father—or someone! No telling what that crazy woman might do!"

Anise ran outside, calling Bonnie's name as loudly as she could, but there was no response. Within a few minutes Clay and the Mortons came back in the jeep. Clay said that Bart could take care of Carl now, while the rest of them searched for Melanie and the little girls. As they fanned out in different directions, Anise took the trail where she and Bonnie had walked this morning, the trail Greg had said was safe.

The children were not in the garden, and she couldn't find them in the woods. She continued to call until she was hoarse, but there was still no response. When she came to the fork in the trail where it joined the narrow road up to the forbidden quarry, she paused and tried to quiet the wild hammering of her heart. Surely the children wouldn't go up there! Yet remembering how Laura had dared Bonnie to go into a dangerous surf, Anise knew it was entirely possible that she had challenged her to take another risk. Then there was Melanie— poor crazed Melanie—who had turned against her own child, and doubtless had no love for Sylvia's daughter either.

Anise gazed down the trail that led to the beach. The little girls could have gone that way, of course. That is, if they had followed this trail at all. Yet something forced her feet inexorably up the quarry road. Call it intuition or logic, or simply dumb panic, she thought, she couldn't go on until she had searched out this dangerous possibility.

The rocky, weed-strewn road led upward in zigzag fashion through a forest. It was so steep that she was soon out of breath, and had to stop and pant for a few minutes before she could get enough air to call Bonnie's name.

Once when she called, she thought she heard a faint response somewhere far above. She redoubled her efforts until it seemed her lungs would burst with the strain. When she was finally forced to pause for breath, and to let the painful thumping of her heart subside a little, she heard running, skidding footsteps coming down the road.

She had thought she couldn't move another step, but now, as if with second wind, she found her feet carrying her upward, while her expanding heart and lungs gave her new energy.

Rounding the next curve, she saw Laura catapulting toward her, barely keeping to her feet as her arms flailed wildly. Her voice came out in a high thin wail.

"Miss Weston! Help! Hurry! My mother pushed Bonnie over into the quarry and I can't get her out!"

Anise felt her knees buckle with fear as she remembered what Greg had said about the abandoned quarry. Steep sides lined with gravel and loose shale that could bury anyone who fell into it!

"Oh, Bonnie. Oh, Bonnie," she moaned, forcing her trembling knees to carry her on up the road. Laura was sobbing beside her, chattering between breathless sobs as she tried to explain what happened. Anise could hardly listen. It took all the force she could muster just to keep hurrying up that rough road.

Finally they reached the top. She saw the yawning chasm where rock had been quarried from one whole side of the hill. Bonnie was nowhere in sight.

Melanie was on her hands and knees, peering over the edge. Her hair hung in tangled strands, her printed housecoat was torn off one shoulder and hung in tatters.

"Don't let her get me!" Laura cried, grabbing Anise by the arm. "She'll push me over, too! She tried to—but I kicked and fought! Should I go find somebody to help us?"

Anise paused, her hand pressed against the throbbing pulse at her throat as she tried to catch her breath and think what to do.

"Yes, go get help!" she told Laura. "Get your Uncle Clay and the Mortons. Tell them to hurry—and bring a rope or something!"

"Don't let my mother push you!" Laura whimpered. "She's crazy! She made us come here. We didn't want to!"

"Go on!" Anise said, taking her by the shoulders to face her

113

downward on the road. "Hurry as fast as you can! I'll see what I can do for Bonnie—but we've got to have help!"

"Don't fall!" Laura cried over her shoulder as she started running down the road, her feet skidding in loose gravel.

Anise had been keeping her eyes on Melanie, but the woman hadn't moved. She seemed unaware that Anise was there, or that Laura had been talking. She appeared to be in a trance as she remained rigidly kneeling, staring down into the pit.

"Melanie . . ." Anise spoke softly, moving closer. She wondered how strong the woman was. If they had to fight, would Melanie be powerful enough to force her over the edge of the quarry? Melanie was in danger herself as she knelt there, so close to the gravelly brim.

"Melanie . . ." Anise repeated, moving still closer.

This time the woman became aware of her. With a startled cry, she scrambled to her feet and backed away from the quarry, her eyes wide and mouth stretched in panic.

"Sylvia!" she quavered. She covered her face with trembling hands and swayed dizzily.

"I'm not Sylvia," Anise said in a soothing tone. "Look at me and you'll see!"

Melanie's hands dropped away from her face, but the fear was still there. Her eyes bulged, her mouth twisted out of shape, baring her teeth.

"Don't tell him, Sylvia! I won't let you! I'll kill you before I'll let you tell him! I'll kill you!" She came toward Anise sobbing, her arms thrust forward, fingers curved as if to clutch her by the throat.

Anise caught the woman's hands and thrust her aside. Melanie sprang toward her again, snarling. For long, panting moments they were locked in a writhing embrace.

"You didn't believe him, Sylvia!" Melanie taunted. "I knew you wouldn't! Because you're a shrew! A jealous shrew! You don't deserve him!"

"Stop it, Melanie—I'm not Sylvia!" Anise cried, struggling to free herself. She kept pulling the clinging arms loose, only to feel them close around her again. And always there was that yawning pit toward which Melanie kept pushing her. Unable to keep her eyes on it, Anise had the horrified feeling that at any moment they might both go plunging over.

Suddenly Melanie reared back and stared at her, screaming

114

hysterically. Her fingers dug into the soft flesh above Anise's elbows, making her gasp with pain.

"You're dead!" Melanie shrieked. "How can you be here when you're dead! Now I'll never be rid of you!"

Looking ready to faint, Melanie backed away, then turned and went plunging past to run wildly down the road. Her thin shrill wail floated on the air behind her.

Anise felt every muscle tremble as she moved slowly toward the ragged, pebbly brink of the quarry.

"Bonnie—" she quavered, her voice almost too weak now to make a sound.

To her relief, there was an answer. A faint, bleating cry somewhere below. Crawling on hands and knees, Anise moved close enough to peer over the edge.

Hardly six feet down, Bonnie was clinging to a sharp projection, surrounded by a landslide of loose shale and gravel. The sharp rock had fortunately protruded far enough for the child to grab hold as she fell. She looked tiny, frail and frantic as she clung there, sobbing.

"Bonnie!" Anise gasped on a deep breath of relief. "Hang on, honey! Laura's gone for help."

"I'm trying to hang on," Bonnie whimpered. "But my hands keep slipping. It's all loose under my feet and I can't climb back up there."

"Don't try to yet," Anise cautioned, realizing that any movement by the child might cause further sliding of the gravel around and above her, sweeping her off the ledge, down into the pit where she would be buried.

"It's slippery," Bonnie wailed. "And my hands are so tired!"

They couldn't wait for help, Anise decided. She would have to do something herself. She got up and searched the area frantically. A short distance into the woods she saw a limb that might be long enough. About two inches in diameter at its thickest point, it had a broken branch projecting that looked sturdy enough for Bonnie to get a firm hold, if it would only reach her.

Carrying it back to the brink, she peered over and found Bonnie still handing on, sobbing weakly.

"Bonnie, see if you can get hold of this," Anise said, lowering the limb to her. For a moment she was afraid it wouldn't reach, or that her own end would be too thin and fragile to bear the child's weight. But on bending it, she found it tough

115

and unbreakable clear to the twiggy end, so she knew she had to take the chance. Bonnie's position looked much too precarious.

"Can you hang on to this?" she asked, peering down into Bonnie's frightened little face. She saw the small fingers transfer their grip, one hand at a time, to the limb and its projecting branch.

"I've got it," Bonnie gasped. "I'll hang on tight."

Anise began to pull firmly upward. Bonnie's feet could get no purchase on the loose, sliding gravel, and the child's weight seemed tremendous. Anise lay face down on the ground, feeling as if her arms were being wrenched from their sockets as she tried not to let herself slide forward.

The edge of the pit began to break away beneath her. She worked her way backward slowly, painfully, the downward drag on her arms making her shoulders numb. Then, hand over hand, making inch by inch progress, she pulling the limb upward. She was sobbing with the effort when at last Bonnie's little hands were within reach of hers. She grabbed one wrist, then the other.

"See if you can dig your feet in now," she begged. "Help me get you over the top."

One last desperate strain, and Bonnie scrambled up to safety. Anise caught her in her arms and for a long moment they both lay on the ground, breathless and trembling.

"Bonnie, what happened?" Anise asked when finally she could breathe normally, and her trembling began to subside. Her arms still ached with the strain, but that didn't matter, now that Bonnie was safe. "How on earth did you get down there? Did somebody push you?"

"The board slipped and I fell with it," Bonnie said shakily.
"What board?"

"There was a board along the edge. Laura got on it on her knees and looked over the edge. She said there were goblins down there. Her mother looked too and said they weren't goblins, they were only little sprites and bogeys like us. Laura called me a scaredy-cat because I didn't want to look down and see. So I did. And the board slipped." She shuddered and burrowed closer in Anise's arms.

"Laura said her mother pushed you," Anise said.

Bonnie glanced up at her, seeming puzzled. "Maybe she

pushed the board, and I thought it just slid. She was right there."

"Where was Laura?"

Bonnie frowned. "I don't know. She yelled for me to be careful, but I was already falling."

"Did they try to help you climb out?"

Bonnie pondered that for a moment. "I don't think so. I think they just kept on fighting."

"You mean they were quarreling? What about?"

Bonnie shrugged. "I don't know. It sounded sort of crazy. Laura says her mother really is crazy."

"She is, Bonnie. Do you know how she got out of her room?"

Bonnie shook her head. "Laura thought she heard her and went down the hall. When she came back, her mother came too and said we should all take a walk. Laura said we'd better do what she said or she'd go wild."

"Do you know who unlocked her door? Deirdre said she left her locked in."

"No." Bonnie scrambled to her feet. "Let's get away from here. I'm still scared. Can't we drive back to that place where we got off the airplane, and fly away? Let's not wait for my daddy to come back. Let's just *go!*"

Anise sighed and stood up, finding her knees still shaky. "I'm afraid it isn't that simple, honey. But I'll see what I can do about it."

No one was in sight as they walked through the garden and approached the house. A moment later Clay came running from the cliff path shouting, then Mr. and Mrs. Morton appeared from a different direction, while Deirdre and Miss Enid came rushing out of the house.

"Thank God, Bonnie's safe!" Clay exclaimed, hurrying toward them. "Where was she? And where are Melanie and Laura?"

"Aren't they here yet?" Anise gasped. "You mean you don't know what happened?"

His expression darkened as she explained about the accident at the quarry, and his brow furrowed with anxiety.

"They should never have been there!" he said, shaking his head. "Laura knows better."

"Of course they shouldn't have been there!" Anise agreed hotly. "And I'm sure it wasn't Bonnie's idea to run into such

117

danger. Laura's always daring her to do something she shouldn't. I wouldn't be a bit surprised if she or Melanie, or both, shoved that board over the edge with Bonnie on it!"

"No!" Clay exclaimed, then amended hastily. "Maybe Melanie did. I wouldn't put anything past—"

"She wouldn't do anything like that!" Mrs. Morton broke in. "She may be off her rocker, but she's not vicious!"

"I wouldn't think so ordinarily, but. . . ." Clay turned back to Anise. "Maybe the edge just gave way. It's pretty crumbly in places, that's why it's so dangerous. We may never know unless. . . . Where are Laura and her mother now? Good Lord, we've got to find them before something happens. Melanie has become so hostile to her child there's no telling what—"

He broke off as his glance went beyond them. Turning to follow his gaze, Anise saw Laura running down the path from the reservoir.

"Mother's trying to climb the fence and jump in!" Laura cried as she rushed through the gate. "I can't make her come home!"

"We'll get her!" Mr. Morton said as he and his wife both hurried off.

Anise turned to Laura. The child looked bedraggled, her round freckled face smudged with dirt and tears, her taffy blonde hair matted with pine and fir needles, her dress torn. She was panting noisily.

"Laura, you were supposed to come and find help for Bonnie," Anise said sternly. "Why didn't you?"

"I tried to," Laura wailed, giving in to fresh tears. "My mother wouldn't let me! She hurt me! I think she wants to kill me! Like she tried to kill Bonnie!"

"Poor baby," Clay said, picking the child up in his arms. "You're all upset. Your mother's sick, you know. She doesn't really mean everything she says or does. She can't help herself."

"She was supposed to be locked in her room," Anise said. "Bonnie couldn't tell me how she got out."

"That's right!" Deirdre chimed in. "I locked that door before I went up to the cottage. I'd like to know who unlocked it!"

"Laura, did you?" Anise asked, watching the child closely.

118

Laura shook her head and buried her face against Clay's shoulder.

"Of course, she didn't!" Clay snapped. "How could she, without a key? Deirdre probably just thought she locked it. She's been careless before." He turned to the girl. "You were in a hurry to leave for the cottage when you heard about Carl. I bet you didn't turn the key all the way around."

"Yes, I did," Deirdre mumbled, her face flaming red. "But now I can't find the key. It must've slipped out of my pocket."

"You see?" Clay turned triumphantly to Anise. "Anyone could have found it and unlocked that door! So don't try to blame it on an innocent child!"

"Then you tell me who it was!" she demanded angrily. "There are just too many unexplained accidents happening around here. I want to take Bonnie away. She has decided she would rather live with her grandparents, and I'm sure she'd be safer with them. Will you drive us to the airport?"

"Azbsolutely not!" His face was grim over Laura's blonde head. "Do you want Greg to skin me alive? And don't try to bribe anyone else around here to drive you there either! Greg would have us all strung up by our thumbs. He's longed for this little daughter ever since she was born. It would be worth our lives to let her get away now."

He laid his free hand on her shoulder. "Don't be frightened, honey. Greg will be home in a few days. Meanwhile, we'll all pitch in and try to keep closer watch over both Melanie and Bonnie. We all love the child." His eyes took on a warmer glow as he added softly, "We love you, too, Anise."

Anise took Bonnie's hand and walked dispiritedly into the house. Escape looked pretty hopeless, but she wouldn't give up. The first chance she got, she would try again to persuade Mr. Morton to drive them to the airport.

CHAPTER 12

She had no chance to talk to Mr. Morton alone during the next few days. She tried to keep Bonnie pleasantly occupied, and never let the child out of her sight. She went with her to the classroom, refusing to let her stay afterward to play with Laura. They took brief walks on the beach or in the garden, but never wandered far from the house. When fog rolled in, they spent hours playing games or reading in their rooms.

They were playing Scrabble late one afternoon when they heard the plane drone in. The fog had lifted, so they had spent the early afternoon on the beach. Anise had suggested a walk afterward, but Bonnie shuddered and shook her head.

"Let's just go to our rooms. I feel better there."

Now, as the roar of the jeep's motor followed the descent of the plane, Anise suggested going down to greet her father.

The child seemed to cringe. "Do we have to go now? We'll see him at dinner, won't we?"

"Yes, I suppose so, but I thought you might want to see him right away. We should feel safer now that he's home."

Bonnie frowned, then rubbed her forehead. "I'd rather finish our game first. I can beat Laura at Scrabble so she never wants to play it anymore. She tips the board over, or messes up the tiles when I get ahead."

"She's not a very good sport, is she? All right, we'll finish our game."

Bonnie had read a great deal, and had a large vocabulary for her age. Anise seldom had to correct her spelling either. Now as the child pondered thoughtfully over each word, the game lasted until time to get ready for dinner.

Again Anise found herself taking extra care with her dressing and grooming. She scoffed at her vanity as she peered into the mirror to apply a touch of mascara to her naturally long brown lashes. She had Bonnie change from her play slacks into a navy blue jumper with a ruffled white blouse.

"All ready to meet royalty," she said as they went out into the hall.

Bonnie smiled up at her. "Maybe my daddy will teach me how to swim tomorrow. I'd almost forgotten about that."

The family had already gathered in the dining room. Dinner was served in style, Anise thought whimsically, now that the lord of the manor had returned.

Greg dominated the conversation from the start. After greeting Anise and Bonnie, he asked Bonnie what she had been doing with herself. She seemed too shy to answer, so he turned to adult talk about the mill, discussing its problems with Clay.

Anise found herself fascinated all over again as she listened to the quiet modulations of his voice, saw the play of emotions across his countenance, darkening it at times, then brightening as he smiled over the details of some small victory over men or machines in what sounded like a thriving lumber industry.

When the meal was finished, he smiled at Bonnie and said, "You children can be excused while the rest of us have a last cup of coffee. Go up to Laura's playroom and have a good time. I'll be up to see you later."

Seeing Bonnie's face grow noticeably pinched and pale, Anise said, "I'll go with them. I—"

"No, you stay here." His tone was peremptory.

"I don't like sending Bonnie off without me. I've been keeping close watch over her ever since—"

"So I've heard," he broke in dryly, his frown bringing his eyebrows down to the winglike slant that gave him an almost satanic expression. "I want to talk to you about that. If Enid goes along you surely can't find anything to worry about." He nodded at Miss Enid who promptly got up and took each child by the hand to herd them from the room.

121

"Now," Greg said, turning to Anise after Miss Enid and the children were out of hearing. "I want your version of this accident up at the quarry."

She told him exactly as she remembered each detail, and watched the furrow deepen between his eyebrows.

"That tallies," he said, nodding. His mouth was still grim. "Then you have no proof it was anything but a simple accident?"

"I told you, Laura said her mother pushed Bonnie over!"

He shook his head. "I've questioned her, and Laura admits now she could have been mistaken. She was hysterical at the time, and afraid of her mother. She's pretty sure now that the edge crumbled and the board gave way."

"Or else she shoved Bonnie herself."

Greg looked aghast. "You can't be serious! Laura's just a child! She has looked forward eagerly to having a sister here to play with. Why would she do a vicious thing like that to her? It doesn't make sense!"

"Nothing makes sense around here!" Anise cried, almost tearful in her frustration. "Bonnie hates it! She wants to go live with her grandparents. We both want to leave, but nobody will drive us to the airport!"

"I told you about that," Clay put in mildly, but Greg ignored him. Keeping his dark gaze on Anise, he spoke coldly, almost contemptuously.

"That's the stupidest thing I've heard from you. This is Bonnie's home, and I've told you exactly how I feel about the Dimmicks. Bonnie is my responsibility, and we all love her, even though she still gives little response."

He paused, and his manner thawed a little as he went on. "I think her problem is that she has been so overprotected she's afraid of her shadow, and that is why she's so accident prone. You're not doing her any good by continuing to treat her like either an invalid or a prisoner. Mrs. Morton says you've hardly been out of your rooms except to skitter to the beach for a minute and right back."

"Can you blame us, when the first time I leave her, she gets dragged up to the quarry, and either fell or was pushed in?"

His eyes were stern. "Did Bonnie tell you she was dragged up there?"

"Well, no, but. . . ." Why did Bonnie go? Anise wondered. She hadn't questioned her closely about that.

"According to Laura," Greg said, "the children went along with the hope of dissuading Melanie from going far. But Melanie was stubborn and quarrelsome. Laura understands her condition, but of course has no means of controlling her, except persuasion. Sometimes that works, but this time it didn't. It's too bad Melanie got out of her room just at that time, when the household was busy elsewhere. I blame Deirdre severely for that, and will probably have to replace her with someone more dependable."

"Meanwhile Bonnie is in danger!" Anise declared.

"No, Mrs. Morton has been taking charge of Melanie since that day, and doing a good job. Now that I'm home, I can help to keep things under control. So I want you to quit pampering Bonnie. Let her live like a normal ten-year-old girl!"

"That's exactly what she is!" Anise retorted. "Any ten-year-old girl would be frightened by the things that have happened to her. I don't think Laura is good company for her, either. She dares her to do things that are dangerous. Calls her scaredy-cat if she refuses."

"That's quite normal for children that age, isn't it?" His tone was milder now, and he was smiling. "Bonnie must learn to stand up for herself, to fend off a foolish challenge like that. Anyway, I'll be spending more time at home now. I'll take her in hand."

"That's a relief," Clay said. "Things run smoother with you around, both here and at the mill. But of course, you can't be in both places at once."

"So it's lucky I have you to help out," Greg replied, grinning at his brother.

"Do you need my help at the mill now?" Clay asked. "Shall I go back tomorrow?"

"No, it won't be necessary. Everything seems okay there now. I'll give the foreman a chance to see if he can handle it alone."

"Good." Clay looked pleased as he settled back in his chair. "Then maybe I'll take off for a couple of days. Is the plane serviced, ready for takeoff?"

"Yes, but you can't use it tomorrow," Greg said sharply. "I'm finally getting a chance to take Bonnie over to the lake to start her swimming lessons."

He smiled at Anise. "We'll want you along, too. Plan for a
123

pleasant holiday to make up for all you and Bonnie have been through. Pack your swimsuits and plenty of towels. I'll gather up any other paraphernalia we'll need, and we'll leave right after breakfast."

"That sounds like fun!" Clay declared. "If the plane had more seats I'd beg to go along. Since you're using it tomorrow, I'd like to preempt it for Saturday night. I've promised to fly Anise down to San Francisco to dance some night, and there's a real swinging lodge affair coming up Saturday." He smiled at Anise. "How about it?"

"That—that would be nice." She felt strangely breathless. Yet she had promised to go, and knew of no reason to refuse. Turning to Greg, she found him studying her quizzically. Then a motion beyond him caught her eye and she glanced up to see Deirdre standing at the door. The girl's face looked pinched, hard, and angry. Her eyes glittered before she shadowed them with her long eyelashes. Approaching Greg she said stiffly, "You rang for me, sir?"

Greg smiled up at her. "Yes, Deirdre, we'd like more coffee all around. If there isn't enough left, make a fresh pot."

"Yes, sir." She gave Anise a brief, hostile glance as she turned on her heel and left the room.

So she thinks I'm beating her time, Anise thought, wondering if she should feel guilty about it. She found Clay staring after the girl reflectively.

"I took Deirdre dancing over at the lake one night," he said, his voice low. "She has so little chance for fun, stuck up here on the coast with no young men around, no parties to attend. But I've been afraid to do anything for her since. She takes too much for granted."

"I told you it was foolish to give her any encouragement," Greg said, "unless you mean it seriously."

"Heaven forbid!" Clay rolled his eyes. "I'm not about to make love to the kitchen maid."

"You needn't be snobbish about it!" Greg chided, his mouth tight again. "I'm sorry for the girl, too, but she's really not very efficient. I think the kindest thing I could do for her is find her a job in some town or city where she'd have friends her own age. But of course, Fannie wants her here where she can keep an eagle eye on her."

His eyes suddenly twinkled at Anise. "That's what comes of this overprotective pampering. You can't stop even when the

124

child has grown up! That's why I want you to foster more independence in Bonnie while she's still a child."

Anise stared at him mutinously, seeking words to make him understand that she was trying to protect his daughter from real danger. He shouldn't call that pampering!

"Well, since we're cutting out all the pampering around here," Bart said, toying with his empty cup, "I hope it's okay if I take Carl skin diving in the morning."

"No!" Greg looked up as Deirdre came in and started pouring coffee. He waited until she had filled each cup, then he went on firmly, "I don't want you taking Carl into the surf again while I'm not home. I don't want him taking another notion to end it all out there."

"Heck, he won't do that now!" Bart declared. "Not after falling in love with that Dobie pup." He turned to Anise, grinning. "You should have seen the way he fought against it at first. He turned his back, refusing even to look at the little black Doberman. But when the puppy whimpered and licked his hand, Carl gave it one glance and couldn't resist. The next minute he had the wriggling little guy in his arms and was crying. They'll be pals now."

"Just the same," Greg said quietly, "you're not to take him skin diving unless I'm here. You have plenty to keep you busy tomorrow. And every day, as far as that goes. Deirdre isn't the only inefficient one around here. If you can't do a better job of keeping an eye on both Carl and Melanie, I'll have to call in a professional."

They stared at each other for a moment, then Bart said, "I wouldn't care if you did, if only you'd give me a job at the mill instead. I mean a real job, not just a flunky."

"Show me you rate a job like that," Greg told him, "and I will someday. First you must prove yourself completely responsible and dependable."

Bart flushed, as if knowing he hadn't quite proven himself yet. He drained his cup then asked to be excused, saying he wanted to go over to the cottage and see how Carl was making out with the pup.

"Stop at the kitchen and see if Fannie wants to send him some dinner." Greg stood up and spoke to Anise. "I'm going to spend some time with the children, then I'll send Bonnie to you. After she's tucked in for the night, come to the living room. I want to talk with you."

About what? Anise wondered as she went up to her room to wait for Bonnie. About half an hour later Bonnie came in, looking flushed and excited.

"We're going to fly to a lake tomorrow!" she exclaimed. "Just you and me and Daddy! Laura can't go and she's mad. And I'm glad!"

Sibling rivalry, Anise thought. She supposed it was quite normal, yet it seemed strange to have sprung up so quickly between two little girls who hadn't grown up together, and still scarcely knew each other. It was as if they sensed instinctively that they were rivals for a father's love and a rich inheritance. Yet Bonnie knew little and cared less about owning property. It was doubtful if Laura really comprehended the wealth of Mendolair, even if her family had for some reason tried to impress her with it.

Anise had kissed Bonnie good-night and was about to leave her room when Greg knocked at the door.

"Put on a light wrap," he said, "and we'll walk out to the cliff. There isn't a wisp of fog tonight, and the moon is brilliant."

The air was crisp and redolent with the fragrance of brine and kelp. She found her wide knitted shawl warm enough as she wrapped it about her and walked beside him.

"I think I made strides in winning Bonnie's confidence tonight," he said, guiding her with a light touch at her elbow as they followed the cliffside path. "She seems eager about tomorrow. And those little girls are becoming more like sisters every time I see them together. Talk about sibling rivalry!"

Anise told him what Bonnie had said, and he chuckled. "I explained to Laura that she had been to the lake with me several times, and will be going again sometime. Tomorrow I want the chance to be with you and Bonnie alone. You're a charming girl, Anise. I want to know you better. I hope I can keep you here a long time."

"You *hope* you can?" she questioned faintly. Was there a hidden threat to dismiss her, as he had more openly threatened to let Bart and Deirdre go? Was this another warning not to be overprotective? He couldn't seem to believe there was any real danger here.

Instead of answering, he came to a halt on the path and took her elbow warmly in his palm. "See how the foam of the cresting waves catches the gleam of moonlight? An artist once told me that a black and silver night scene like this is the hardest thing in the world to paint realistically. He has tried it, but the bright blackness seems impossible to reproduce in any medium. The nearest he has come is by painting with silver on black velvet. But that lacks the gradations of shade and the—well, liveliness, you might say."

Anise knew what he meant. As he fell silent, engrossed in the view, she noted how the promontory rocks caught a paler gleam than the roughened path of moonlight on the ocean where the wind was whipping the ripples into whitecaps.

As they walked on down the path toward the promontory, she glanced up at the lopsided moon and remembered how she had been fascinated by Clay when they were here a few nights ago. She felt almost ashamed of that thrill now that she was here with Greg. Almost a sense of betrayal. Yet why should she? Greg was in no position to make romantic overtures, even if he wanted to. He had a wife, legally, though it was hard to think of Melanie as being his wife in any other way.

Besides, Anise told herself, he had given no indication that he would mind at all if she had a romance with his brother.

Remembering the frightening way her walk with Clay had ended, she asked impulsively, "Did Clay tell you about the night we were shot at up here?"

His hand tensed about her elbow. "Yes," he replied shortly. "He and the Mortons have found empty cartridges that indicate campers must have wandered in from the state park. They do, sometimes. And some crazy hunter mistook you for a deer or something."

"Who'd be foolish enough to hunt in the dark?"

"No one in his right mind, certainly," he agreed. "George says there was an empty whiskey bottle near some of the cartridges, so they were probably drunk. I'm going to have to erect a chainlink fence with a locked gate at the boundry near the park, and extend it up the hill to where the woods become nearly impenetrable."

"Meanwhile," she said, beginning to shiver, "we could be shot at right here!"

"You're cold," he said, putting an arm about her and heading back toward the woods. "We'll go over to the shadow of the trees where you'll feel safer and warmer. We don't have poachers very often. It's unfortunate they happened to be out that night."

127

"They were out that first afternoon Bonnie and I were here, too," she reminded him.

"I know, and I'm sorry. We'll do all we can to see that it doesn't happen again. That was the day Mancho got loose and almost attacked you, too. I'm sorry I couldn't have been here to give you a better reception, and prevent your being so frightened. I guess it's just as well George shot that dog. I hadn't the heart to order it, with Carl so fond of the creature."

"Why do you keep Carl in a place like this?" she asked. "Are you sure it's good for him?"

"It's where he wants to be, and I believe that a kid, as short-changed in life as Carl, should have everything possible to keep him contented. He doesn't need institutional care. He has already had the maximum amount of training, aside from what we can teach him about the work here. If he weren't here, he'd be in a foster home. I think he's better off with his family. Clay and I do what we can for him, too."

His hand was at her elbow again, firm and warm. Pausing in the shadow of tall trees at the edge of the woods, she couldn't see his face clearly. But she felt the thrill of his closeness, and at the moment she liked him better than she had at any time since she first met him. She had to warn herself again not to become emotionally involved with this married man, who probably had no personal interest in her anyway.

"I think it's rather wonderful," she couldn't resist saying, "the way you are taking care of Melanie and her whole family. It seems like a tremendous responsibility."

"Nothing wonderful or tremendous about it," he replied gruffly. "Sometimes I'm afraid I'm just using them. They all help around here, you know. Except Melanie, of course, and she might be better off if I had simply left her in the hospital where she would have professional care. Clay thinks so. But at the time I brought her here she wanted to come, and the doctors thought it might be good for her."

"Melanie told me she thinks you're trying to drive her crazy."

He snorted. "A schizo is likely to say anything. Don't pay any attention to her raving. Just try to take good care of Bonnie without overdoing it. We'd better head back for the house. You're shivering again."

He seemed to be rushing her as his tense hand guided her along the dark path. The friendliness was gone from his manner, and she wasn't sure she liked him so well after all.

128

CHAPTER 13

Anise was walking through a dark forest of tall, gaunt trees covered with moss and festooned with lichens like cobwebs. They kept brushing against her face, making her shudder with revulsion. She opened her eyes and found Bonnie lightly stroking her cheeks.

"Is it time to get ready?" Bonnie asked while Anise fought off the horror of her dream. "Daddy said we'd start right after breakfast."

Anise bounded out of bed. "What time is it?" The room was bright with daylight, but the clock said only five-thirty. She went to the window and saw that golden sunlight had slanted through a gap in the mountain range to sparkle on a calm, delft blue sea.

"What a beautiful day for an outing!" she exclaimed. Not a wisp of fog misted the air. She opened the windows to breathe in the salty fragrance. A cacophony of squawking could be heard from the beach where seabirds had gathered in force to hunt for their breakfast.

"What shall I wear?" Bonnie asked, bringing her mind back to the business at hand.

Bonnie chatted cheerfully as they showered and dressed in sportswear. She seemed more like a normal ten-year-old girl than at any time since her mother's illness. They packed swim-suits, towels and beach jackets, and were ready for the trip by the time the first breakfast bell rang.

Greg seemed in good spirits this morning, too. He was talk-ing with Clay and Bart when Anise entered the breakfast room with Bonnie. He turned to them smiling. "I can hardly picture a finer day for flying and swimming," he said. "Keep your fin-gers crossed so the fog won't roll in and spoil it."

He frowned when Deirdre came in to serve breakfast and said that Laura and Miss Enid had requested service in their rooms.

"Laura's still pouting because she can't go today," Deirdre added.

"I thought I made it clear last night," Greg said, his mouth momentarily tense, "why she can't go. I don't want any dis-tractions while I'm giving Bonnie these first lessons."

He smiled at Bonnie. "You'll be a little water sprite, too, by the time you've learned to swim in quiet water." Glancing at Anise, he said, "I hope you're a good swimmer?"

"Fair," she replied. "I've never won any trophies for speed, but I can stay waterborne indefinitely by floating on my back or treading water, if I get tired of swimming."

He nodded. "That should be sufficient. We won't be racing."

Immediately after breakfast he loaded the jeep with back-rests and a beach umbrella, as well as extra towels and his own swim trunks and jacket. After the brief ride to the airstrip ev-erything was transferred to the little red and white airplane.

Anise had never flown in such a small plane before. As she watched Greg put Bonnie in her seat and fasten the belt, she wondered if the child felt the same trepidation that was begin-ning to make her own pulse race. Bonnie's eyes were bright, her cheeks pink, and her eager questions showed excitement rather than fear.

"Now we'll harnass you in," Greg said, offering Anise his hand. Apparently he noted her slight trembling, for he frowned and asked, "You're not afraid, are you?"

She tried to laugh. "Not really. It's just that I've never been in a private plane before, and it seems so—so sort of small and fragile."

"It's small and light," he agreed, "but that doesn't mean it's either flimsy or fragile. We keep it in good condition, it's easy to handle, and you'll be perfectly safe." His tone dared her to be afraid now.

She didn't try to talk while he revved the motor to warm the engine, studying dials and gauges. She held her breath when he put the plane in motion to taxi along the landing strip that now seemed woefully short to her. Surely they would never be airborne before reaching the row of trees and humping rocks that loomed up ahead, coming closer and closer. . . .

She scarcely felt the rise of the plane, but amazingly the rocks and trees slid safely beneath them, and only the bright blue sky was in sight ahead. Bonnie squealed with delight, and Anise began to breathe again.

As he leveled off to circle Mendolair, she glanced down at the big house that looked like a castle in the woods beside the rugged coast. From this angle it seemed sprawling rather than tall and narrow, its turrets and cupolas out of their normal perspective. She could pick out the wing where she and Bonnie shared a suite.

As they gained an altitude that gave the mountains and sea the aspect of a relief map, she tried to orient herself to this section of the California coast. Shouting above the roar of the engine, she asked Greg the name of a cape coming into view. He started to answer, then broke off short, his eyes startled just before they were shadowed by a heavy scowl.

At the same moment, she became aware of a difference in the sound of the motor. It seemed to miss a chug or two, sputtered and spit, gave a sort of cough, then there was no sound at all. Just ominous silence.

Quick terror caught like pain at her chest as they plunged downward. Or was that sinking sensation only the result of her fear? The small plane was still high above the earth, carried onward by momentum and the spread of its wings.

"What the devil. . . ." Gregory growled, scowling at the instrument panel as he maneuvered the controls. She tried to ask him what was the matter, but fear constricted her throat so she couldn't speak—could scarcely breathe.

"The plane doesn't make that big noise anymore," Bonnie complained in a small shaky voice. "Are we there already? Are we going to land?"

"Not if I can help it," Greg murmured through tight lips, concentrating on the controls. He was heading toward the ocean now and Anise was gripped with new terror. Were they

131

going to go down in the water? Did he consider that less hazardous than crash-landing in the mountains? The thought was almost more frightening to her, yet as she looked down at the rugged timberland below she knew that crashing into the forest would mean almost certain death.

Smothering a wail that tried to rise to her throat, she reached for Bonnie and pulled her as close as their seatbelts would allow. The child began to whimper.

"Don't cry!" Greg snapped. "Just sit tight."

"I'm scared!" Bonnie sobbed. Anise felt the small body tremble. Disregarding her own fright, then, she found her voice and tried to soothe Bonnie's fears with comforting words.

Suddenly Greg banked the plane and changed direction to follow the craggy coastline.

"What are you doing?" she quavered. This seemed the most dangerous place of all to crash. They were right above the rocky cliffs where great waves dashed in with the full tide. Even as she gazed down, horrified, however, she felt a sharp jolt as the plane seemed to zoom upward.

"Ah . . . " Greg gave a sigh that sounded like relief. "We caught an updraft from the cliffs. I've had glider training, this plane might be light enough . . . and I know the topography. . . ."

Again he was busy at the controls, pausing only to bark into the microphone, apparently briefing the tower control somewhere on their plight and location. His face was tight as he concentrated. Did he think he could pull them out of this—somehow reach safety?

For what seemed hours—but she suspected was only minutes—they flew on in silence except for the wind that buoyed them up in jerks and jolts. Yet they weren't gaining altitude, and fear ran like ice water down her spine, constricting her chest, paralyzing her arms as she clung to Bonnie. The child had buried her face against Anise's shoulder to smother the panting whimpers she couldn't suppress.

When Anise thought she couldn't bear the suspense another moment, she heard Greg speak into the microphone, asking the tower control at the county airport for permission to make a deadstick landing.

"Can we make it?" she asked, trying to keep her voice steady. She felt perspiration cold on her brow, and found her

132

hands clenched so tight that her fingernails dug into her palms. Forcing herself to let go, she struggled to relax and summon a smile for Bonnie's sake. The child was gazing up at her in new anxiety.

"We've got to make it!" Greg's voice was as harsh as his stony profile. Still busy with the controls, he went on jerkily, "Sit tight! Don't panic. I think we have enough altitude to clear the last rise."

They left the cliffs and slanted inland. She hoped the wooded ridge ahead was the last rise. Even so, they seemed to be sinking fast as they approached. She wondered if they could possibly clear the tops of those tall trees . . .

For a long moment she thought they weren't going to make it. She held Bonnie tight, shut her eyes, and braced herself for the crash. When she opened her eyes, the trees were behind and a flat field lay ahead where people, trucks and cars seemed to be converging from every direction.

Seeing the ground rise up, she instinctively hid her face and breathed a frantic, tremulous prayer.

There was a jolt, a series of bumps, then Greg was tugging at her belt. "Come on—get out!" he snapped. "Both of you! If we're not out of fuel there could be a fire. I couldn't quite make the runway, so we dragged a bit."

The next moment they were out of the plane, but nothing happened. No explosion, no fire. Anise breathed easier as Greg led them to a car that had driven up. He spoke to the driver, then to Anise. "Go over to the waiting room while we check the motor and fuel. There's a counter over there where you can get something to eat."

"You think we can eat?" she asked, "the way my stomach turned over? But you did a wonderful job of bringing us in," she added fervently. "Thank you, Greg!"

He grinned and nodded. "We were lucky. Our initial altitude and momentum, plus the currents along the cliffs, gave us enough lift to get us over the hump."

About an hour later he came into the waiting room, his mouth tight, his eyebrows slanted by a heavy scowl. At sight of Anise and Bonnie, he relaxed.

"How about a cup of coffee?" he asked, heading for the counter. "Your stomach should be right-side-up by now."

"What was the matter with the plane?" she asked after he had ordered coffee for them and chocolate for Bonnie.

133

"Nothing was wrong with the plane, and the landing did no damage either. I've checked it over with two mechanics, and all systems are go."

She stared at him and felt her heart quicken with the sickening implications of that. Her skin prickled with the ominous sense of alarm that had grown all too familiar since they came to Mendolair. "Then—then what. . . ."

His mouth tightened and sharp lights sparked in his narrowed dark eyes. "We were out of fuel. The tank's absolutely dry. Yet I filled it late yesterday afternoon when I got home. And the gauge showed full this morning. It was stuck there."

Her hands grew colder. "That means someone . . . someone deliberately. . . ."

He nodded. "Someone drained the tank and tinkered with the gauge. Someone who wanted us to crash. Can you think who it might be?"

"Now maybe you'll believe me!" she cried. "You thought I was making it all up! You accused me of being overprotective! I was just trying to keep Bonnie from being killed! And myself, too! Now someone has tried to kill all three of us! You'd better get busy and figure out who it is!"

He set his jaw hard. "There's one thing this proves beyond all doubt. You've been inclined to accuse Laura of maliciously trying to harm Bonnie. She certainly couldn't be guilty of draining a tank and fixing that gauge so it would read full! I hope you'll be kinder to the child now, and encourage Bonnie to trust her too."

Anise had to agree that Laura could have had nothing to do with this episode. In fact, in each case where she or Bonnie, or both, had been in danger, an older person present was as likely to have been responsible. It was foolish to suspect a child simply because she had an unpleasant personality. That could be due to her haphazard upbringing, her mother being a mental case, her busy father absent so much that Laura was left to the care of relatives and her unattractive governess. Perhaps with more loving discipline, and sympathetic understanding, she could overcome the spoiling of those early years. Anise resolved to give the child more attention and try to gain her confidence.

"Can we still go to the lake and swim?" Bonnie asked as she finished her chocolate and wiped foamy whipped cream from her mouth.

"Of course!" Greg replied. "We won't let the delay spoil our fun." Turning to Anise he added, "I've got to investigate this, but I doubt if we'd gain anything by going home now, unless. . . . What I wish is that we could walk in unannounced and see who is most surprised at our safe return. But the sound of the plane will give plenty of time for dissembling. I suppose what I had better do is hire a professional investigator. Bring a good one there on some pretext, so he can look the situation over before anyone knows why he's there."

"Then you do agree," she said gravely, "that someone is trying to get rid of Bonnie? Probably someone who knows the terms of your will."

His face darkened. "I haven't told anyone but you. However, they may all surmise my intentions. Except Enid. She doesn't know a thing, but the rest know there's no reason why I shouldn't—" He broke off and remained tight-lipped for a moment, then shrugged.

"Come on, let's go. We've lost too much of this sunny day already."

It was a relief to hear the engine running smoothly again, and feel the strong lift as the little aircraft took off from an entirely adequate airstrip. Within half an hour they were landing on a smaller field, and renting a car to drive a short distance to the lake resort.

It was more of a recreational area than Anise had expected. Cabanas, hot-dog stands, and carnival type amusements were scattered along the sandy beach. Behind them were spacious campgrounds among the trees crowded with campers, tents, and trailers.

For an hour Anise alternated between swimming vigorously in the chilly water, and sunning herself on the warm sand. Meanwhile Greg concentrated on teaching his daughter to swim. They didn't seem to tire, or to mind the coldness of the lake water, so Anise finally propped herself against a backrest under the umbrella and read one of the magazines Greg had brought along.

At times she laid the magazine aside and watched Greg play with Bonnie out in the shallow water, or carry her on his shoulders out where it was deeper. Bonnie seemed to be thoroughly enjoying it, all fear and distrust of her father gone now. Once when he picked her up, she flung her arms about his neck and kissed him.

135

For a few blissful, dreamy moments Anise thought how nice it would be if the three of them could be alone at Mendolair, with a few servants they could trust to carry on the work. . . .

She brought herself up short with a scathing reminder that Greg had a wife. He also had another child, and he felt a strong obligation to take care of his wife's family.

I'm the one who doesn't fit into the picture, she told herself firmly. As soon as she was sure Bonnie would be safe, she had better leave. She was becoming prey to too many romantic notions about Gregory Lockwood!

But would she ever be sure Bonnie could be safe here? Certainly not until Greg discovered which one of his wife's family was trying to profit by getting rid of the child.

Who *would* profit most if Laura inherited, instead of Bonnie? Melanie, of course, but did she have sense enough to know it? Perhaps her insanity was faked for the very purpose of disposing of this threat without being discovered. Yet somehow that didn't seem likely. Would her brother or her cousins be able to get their hands on the fortune through her and Laura? Greg had said Bonnie would inherit because Melanie's family had too much influence over Laura. Which members of the family did he mean?

Miss Enid could hardly expect to gain anything from Bonnie's death. And Carl probably had no idea what it was all about. Clay could gain nothing through Laura or Melanie. Besides, he'd already had his share of his father's fortune.

Anise was almost asleep when a spattering of water and scattering of sand announced that Greg and Bonnie had joined her under the umbrella.

"I'm hungry!" Bonnie declared. "Daddy says we can buy hot dogs and ice cream cones and have a picnic!"

Greg shook his dark wet hair back and grinned. "That's for Bonnie," he said. "What would you like? We can dress and go to a pretty good restaurant across the lake."

She shook her head. "I'd rather stay here and settle for a hot dog and an ice cream cone. Plus a mug of coffee."

"Good!" Greg patted her knee. "A gal after my own heart!"

She was helplessly thrilled by the compliment. Right now he was someone she would love to be with forever. Tall, bronzed by the sun, his mouth slanted with laughter, the brooding darkness of his eyes had vanished and they gleamed softly with love whenever they rested on Bonnie. Again Anise thought wishfully how exciting it would be if he were free to love her, too . . . and should miraculously do so.

Watching him walk across the sand to the nearest hot-dog counter, Bonnie clinging to his hand and running to keep up with his long strides, Anise made up her mind to get him to talk more about himself. She wanted to know what sort of man he really was, why he had those dark moods, what sort of life he had lived before she knew him. Maybe there was something in his past that would put an end to this silly feeling that she was falling in love with him.

She found it wasn't easy, however, to get him to talk about himself. He played games with Bonnie, told her stories, promised to take them both to see his mill and ride through the forests where his men were cutting timber. He talked about Bonnie's swimming, and, when an hour had passed after lunch, they went out for her to practice some more.

"She's doing fine," he said when they came back from a long session. Bonnie threw herself face down on the beach towel. "A few more lessons and she'll be ready to challenge her little sister."

"*Little* sister!" Anise teased. "She's bigger than Bonnie!"

"She's fatter. But younger." His face suddenly lost its glow, and his voice became harsh. Anise remembered the circumstances of Laura's birth as the Dimmicks had reported it. Melanie was pregnant with Laura while Sylvia was in the hospital giving birth to Bonnie. So there couldn't be more than a few months difference in their age.

Her mind went back to something Clay had told her one night, sounding bitter. She would like to hear Greg's version of it, especially after the way he had now become somber at mention of Laura's age.

Noticing that Bonnie's eyelids had fluttered shut and the child breathed as if she had fallen asleep, fatigued no doubt, from her unusual exercise, Anise decided to take the plunge.

"Clay told me something about Melanie," she began diffidently, and I've been wondering—"

She broke off as Greg turned to her, such concern in his eyes she was almost afraid to go on.

"What did Clay tell you?" he prompted as her pause lengthened.

She drew a deep breath and searched her memory, wanting to recall the details accurately. Now that the hawklike sharp-

137

ness had come back to his face, she wished she hadn't started this after all. Yet she did want to get his reaction to Clay's accusations. Both men fascinated her, each in his own way, but the antagonism between them made her feel that one was right, one was wrong, and she couldn't decide which. Perhaps the antagonism was mostly on Clay's side. She was anxious to probe Greg's attitude and find out.

"You remember when I told you that Melanie said you were trying to drive her crazy? You said a schizo was likely to say anything. But one night Clay said the same thing, and he seemed disturbed about it. He thought keeping her in . . . well, he called it a Godforsaken place, too far from her psychiatrist, was all wrong."

"Hogwash!" he exclaimed angrily. "That has nothing to do with her condition, and Clay knows it! What else did he say?"

Should she go on? His tone was demanding now, and his eyes probed hers so deeply she felt he would know she was lying if she tried to say there was nothing else.

"He said you wouldn't let him talk to her because. . . . He seemed to think it was because he and Melanie were engaged once. Is that true?"

"Go on," he snapped. "What else did he say?"

She wished more than ever she hadn't brought up the subject. He was once again the darkly brooding man who had practically forced his way in to talk to his ex-wife, upsetting her at a time when she was desperately ill.

"Go on," he repeated when she still hesitated.

"He said then you came on the scene and seduced her, broke up their romance and married her yourself as soon as Sylvia got a divorce. Then he thinks your domineering ways drove Melanie out of her mind, and you insisted on trying to handle it yourself, instead of getting a psychiatrist or something. . . ."

Her words trailed off as she tried to remember whether or not Clay had said anything else. She decided she had told Greg enough, however. Probably too much, judging by the hard set of his jaw, the glower of his eyes. She should have realized this was none of her business and he wouldn't want to talk about it. Probably all she had accomplished was to provoke further hostility between the brothers. Yet, now that she had started, she was determined to know the truth.

He was silent for so long she finally asked, "Is it true about

138

—about their romance?" She couldn't ask if he had seduced Melanie and dumped Sylvia, the way Clay had expressed it. Greg probably wouldn't admit it if true, but if it weren't true, surely he would deny it!

He didn't deny it, and he was no longer glaring at her. His gaze was out over the lake, and as she stared at his grim profile she knew, with a keen sense of disappointment, that she had been wishing with all her heart he would deny the accusation. That was no doubt the only reason she had brought herself to ask him. She had wanted to hear him say it wasn't true. She had wanted him to explain what had actually happened, and exonerate himself completely. But he wasn't going to do it.

She remembered then that Clay had cautioned her against letting anyone know he had told her about it. Especially Greg, he had said. She should have kept still. For now, with a sinking sensation at the pit of her stomach, she realized she had lost her new-found confidence in Greg.

When at last he spoke, he said harshly, "Clay would do better to keep still about our family affairs."

He took his watch from the beach bag and snapped it on his wrist. Glancing at the time, he said dryly, "We'd better be starting back. Bonnie can finish her nap after we get home."

CHAPTER 14

Greg was gentle with Bonnie as he woke her and told her it was time to fly home. He took a bottle of sunburn lotion from his bag and handed it to Anise. "Her cheeks and shoulders look a bit sunburned. Better take this to the cabana and use it before she puts on her clothes. You may need some yourself."

Bonnie slept on the flight home, and Greg was silent most of the way. When he spoke at all it was about altimeter readings, omni stations, ailerons—aeronautical jargon she scarcely comprehended. He seemed determined not to let their conversation touch on personal subjects again. She was glad when at last he circled Mendolair and set the plane down on the small landing strip.

"We won't check and service the plane now," he said as he transferred their beach equipment to the jeep. "It will be safer to do that just before takeoff until I find out what's going on around here."

No one was in sight as they went into the entrance hall. Greg carried their gear upstairs and said, "You'll have an hour or so to rest, then be sure you come down to dinner as soon as the gong rings. I'll be interested in each person's reaction to the sight of us home safe and sound. Though I suppose they all heard the plane and the jeep."

The first member of the household Anise saw was Deirdre. The maid came into the room just about the time Anise figured she had rested long enough and should get herself and Bonnie ready for dinner.

"Oh, so you're home already," Deirdre said, looking surprised but not very concerned. "I came to see if there's any laundry in your hamper."

"Didn't you hear us fly in?" Anise asked.

"I heard a plane when I was up at the cottage. But lots of planes have been flying around today, so I wasn't sure it was you. And I don't remember hearing the jeep. I didn't think you'd be home before dark. I'd better be sure Mom knows you're here for dinner." She ducked into the bathroom and came out with a bag of laundry.

Anise and Bonnie were ready to go downstairs by the time the gong sounded. Bonnie's shoulders and cheeks were quite pink from sunburn, but on the whole she seemed to have benefitted from her excursion. Her eyes were bright, her little face eager as she said she was hungry.

Greg was alone in the dining room. He glanced up sharply as they came in, then relaxed. "I'm glad you came down early," he said. "You can note reactions. Who has seen you so far?"

"Deirdre, and she was going to tell her mother."

He nodded. "The women could scarcely be involved, but I'm not so sure about George." He smiled at Bonnie. "How do you feel by now? All sunburned and tired out?"

"I feel good," she replied. "When can we go again?"

His smile grew tight at the edges. "That depends on a number of things. I don't want to have to make an emergency landing next time."

He seemed about to say more, but Clay and Bart could be heard talking in the entrance hall. A moment later they came into the dining room, looking neither surprised nor puzzled.

"Hi!" Clay said. "Have a good trip?" Without waiting for an answer he grinned down at Bonnie. "Can you swim like a fish?"

"No," she replied gravely, "but I can do a dead-man's float without being scared or getting water in my nose."

"That's a good beginning," Clay agreed, affectionately tousling the child's hair. He glanced up at Greg. "Is the plane serviced, ready to go?"

141

Before Greg could answer, the front door banged and Laura came running in, crying, "Wait for us!" At sight of them all assembled she stopped short and pouted. "I told Miss Enid we'd be late, but she stopped every few minutes."

Miss Enid came in breathlessly. Her face was red, her short hair tumbled, her blouse half out of her waistband. "We only walked as far as the park and back. Laura was determined to go, even though we got a late start. She shouldn't expect me to run all the way home!"

"Take your seats," Greg said dryly. "I'll ring for dinner."

Conversation was casual as they took their places and were served. After Deirdre left the room, Greg spoke across the table to Bart, watching him closely as he asked, "What did you do after dinner last night? Where did you go? Whom did you see?"

"Hey, that sounds like the third degree!" Bart complained, immediately on the defensive. "I didn't take Carl skin diving, if that's what you're hinting. I spent the whole damn evening up at the cottage helping him teach his pup some manners. We're going to name her Lady, hoping she'll learn to act like one."

"Were either George or Fannie at the cottage?" Greg asked.

"George came around a time or two. I guess Fannie was busy with Melanie. George complained that Deirdre should be helping her. But I've an idea I know where Deirdre was." He gave Clay a meaningful glance.

Greg turned to his brother. "How about you? What do you know about all that went on around here last night? What did you do yourself, after dinner?"

Clay raised an eyebrow and shrugged. "What difference does it make? What are you driving at, anyway?"

"Never mind. Just tell me where you went, whom you saw."

Clay shrugged again. "I didn't go anywhere. Don't think I left the house, but I didn't keep a written record of each room I entered. Why the heck do you want to know?"

"Who were you with?" Greg persisted. "What members of the household or staff did you talk with, and when?"

Clay's face began to burn red. "All right," he snapped, "is there any law against my spending a little time with the housemaid? I think Deirdre's a shade or so above the ordinary domestic and she would like to be a nurse, if she could just get

142

out from under her mother's thumb long enough for the training."

"Okay, we'll see what we can do about that," Greg said quietly. "Did you spend the whole evening with her? What time did you leave her?"

"Hell, I don't know! I didn't spend the night with her, if that's what you're worried about. I'm trying to get it across to her that I want to be her friend, but it doesn't mean I have marriage in mind, or even an affair. I want her to understand, well—" He shook his head and scowled.

"In other words," Greg said, and now there was a twinkle in his eye, a teasing grin tugging at his mouth, "you want her to understand that with another attractive young woman in the house, she can't expect to monopolize your romantic attentions, so she needn't get upset about it."

Clay grinned back weakly. "Can you blame me?"

"Maybe not," Greg conceded. "I really didn't mean to pry into your romantic life. I'm just trying to get a picture of where everyone was last night."

"Well, we were in the living room, if that helps," Clay said, beginning to relax. "I don't know where anyone else was. What's up?"

Instead of answering, Greg turned to Miss Enid. "I'd like to know what you did after I left you and Laura."

"My goodness!" She blinked at him, her unattractive face turning pink. "Surely you don't suspect me of—of whatever you suspect somebody of doing last night."

"Just tell me where you were, anyone you talked with, anything you saw."

"But I didn't go anywhere, except to my own room. I didn't see anyone, or hear anything. Well, really, I just can't tell you a thing!"

"All right, Greg," Clay said gravely. "I think you'd better tell us what's bothering you."

Greg was silent for a long moment, his jaw setting hard. "I suppose I might as well spill it, since I don't seem to be getting anywhere asking questions. But don't say anything about it to anyone else until I've had a chance to talk to the others. Somebody tampered with the airplane last night. Or it could have been early this morning before we drove to the hangar. Whoever did it wanted us to crash in the rough timberland between here and the lake."

143

"No!" Clay and Bart spoke at once. Both looked appalled. Anise glanced at Enid and saw her face grow pale.

"You—you mean someone—" Enid stammered, "someone tried to *kill* you all? Oh my! What if Laura and I had gone along!"

"How do you know someone tampered?" Clay asked, frowning. "Couldn't some mechanism have failed after takeoff?"

Greg shook his head. "No mechanism failed. We were out of fuel. The tank could hardly have drained dry by itself, leaving the gauge still reading full."

The brothers stared at each other. Clay looked bewildered. "Golly!" he said, letting out the long breath he had apparently been holding. "I can't figure that. A gauge could get stuck, of course, but— Are you sure you fueled up when you flew home last night?"

"Positive. There's no doubt in my mind that someone went to that hangar and tried to set up a disaster for us. The only question is *who*?"

"Vandals, do you suppose?" Clay suggested. "From the state park? Vandals wouldn't know or care who was going to take the plane up next. Some people are jealous of anyone who can afford planes and estates like this. Or maybe they just needed gas, and it was a coincidence that the gauge went haywire at the same time."

Greg frowned. "I'd like to believe that, but I can't. I'll have to investigate further, and keep my eyes open."

"I hate to tell on George," Bart said hesitantly, "but I'm sure he drove the jeep up to the airstrip last night. At least he drove off in that direction after he'd stopped at the cottage. But I sure can't imagine why he'd want you to crash! He'd lose a good job."

"Maybe he'd expect a better one," Greg said, his mouth tight. "With Bonnie and me out of the picture, everything would go to Melanie. It wouldn't be hard for him to get a court to grant him a conservatorship that would give him complete control."

Bart's jaw dropped. "Hey, I don't think George would do anything like that!" he said shakily, looking awed.

"I wouldn't like to think so either," Greg agreed. "But *somebody*. . . . Anyway, thanks for telling me. I don't want anything said to George about it before I have a chance to talk to him and Fannie. Perhaps right after dinner. If you've all told me all you can, I'll ring for Deirdre to bring dessert."

It was quite late that night, long after Bonnie had gone to sleep, when Greg knocked on the door to ask, "Are you still up, Anise? May I come in for a few minutes?"

She had been reading and was still dressed. She opened the door and invited him in.

"I'm not getting anywhere trying to figure this out by myself," he said, crossing the room to stand at the window. She went over close to him, liking the feeling of strength in his presence. She had been torn by anxiety ever since dinner.

"I think part of my problem," he said, sitting on the window seat and pulling her down beside him, "is the crazy feeling of unreality about the whole thing. When you've expressed fear for Bonnie's life, I've scoffed, because it seemed outlandish to believe that anyone here would harm the child."

"I don't think it's so outlandish, considering your will!"

"But who besides you knows about it? Have you told anyone?"

"Of course not!"

"Not even Bonnie?"

"Especially not Bonnie! She's too young to be worried about property. But I have a feeling that everyone around here knows Bonnie is to be favored. Bart said the family wasn't happy about another heir showing up. They'd thought Sylvia's share had been settled on her long ago."

Greg looked concerned. "When did he say that?"

She told him, adding, "Mr. Morton has been warning us to leave ever since the day we arrived. His wife, too."

"Tell me about it." He took her hand and held it warmly. "Tell me everything that has happened to frighten you since you came here."

It was hard to think straight with her hand cupped in both of his, making her too intensely aware of his nearness. But she went over it all, trying to remember every detail of Mr. Morton's warning on the drive from the airport, his wife's hateful attitude when they arrived at the house. She reported Deirdre saying she was surprised at his bringing Bonnie here, then refusing to say why. She told again of Mancho's attack and her certainty that someone inside the cottage had released him; of

145

the shots that almost hit them as they climbed the ridge to go over to the airstrip.

"Then there were the shots at Clay and me one night," she added, "but Bonnie wasn't with us. Clay thought someone was shooting at him."

"We've pretty much concluded those shots were by drunk poachers," Greg said, dismissing the incident. "You've given me your version of the accident at the quarry, but how about the afternoon Bonnie almost drowned in the surf? It was Enid who warned you of her danger, wasn't it?"

"Yes, but it was her negligence that put Bonnie in danger. Maybe that's why she begged me not to tell anyone she had panicked. She apparently felt embarrassed about it afterward. She seemed to agree with Bart's account of his coming in just in time for the rescue. But if they are in cahoots, he could have been there all the time. My first impression was that he was deliberately trying to drown Bonnie. Until he saw help coming and knew he couldn't get away with it."

"Does that seem likely?" Greg was looking down into her eyes, his own dark and thoughtful. "What would either of them have to gain? That's the trouble, Anise. None of this seems likely, not even the facts we know for sure. What else can you tell me?"

"That's about all, except that I can't figure Miss Enid. One other time she tried to warn me to get Bonnie away from here, but she had no more definite explanation than the Mortons gave. I know you think she's okay, and I'll admit she's a good teacher, but somehow I don't trust her. Did you know that she meets a man up at the park?"

"No! Is it a regular thing?"

"I don't know about that, but Bonnie said she sneaked away from them and got into a car to talk with a man, that day you made me let Bonnie go on a picnic with them. The little girls followed and watched, without Enid knowing. When I told Clay about it, he laughed at the idea of her having a clandestine affair. He said she was probably stopping a trespasser. But Bonnie didn't think that was it. Why would the woman get into the car with a trespasser?"

"I'll do some more checking on her," Greg said, sounding grim. "I thought her references were okay—they sounded good. But maybe I should have double-checked."

146

He fell silent for a few moments, then his hands tightened on hers and he stood up, drawing her with him.

"You're probably wishing I'd leave so you can go to bed and get some sleep."

"I'm not sleepy!" she protested, not wanting him to go. She felt safer in his presence. Then there was something else, a feeling that had started to possess her this afternoon at the lake, the feeling that he belonged with her. In spite of Melanie's existence in another wing of the house, she couldn't repress a tremulous expectancy of something deep and thrilling in their relationship.

"I'm not sure I can sleep even when I go to bed," she added.

"No wonder!" He released her hand and curved an arm about her shoulders, drawing her closer. "With all the frightening things that have happened to you and Bonnie, I don't wonder you're worried! I wish I had wised up sooner. I still feel pretty much in the dark, so I'm going to get some professional help."

He tilted her chin with his finger, and gazed down at her somberly. "That means I'll have to fly to the city tonight. Don't be frightened. There's surely only one person here who poses any danger, and I've put them all to watching each other, so I don't believe anyone will dare try anything while I'm gone."

"I still feel safer when you're here," she murmured. Her heart was pounding. She wasn't sure whether it was fear that shook her, or simply the excitement of being held in the curve of his arm, her gaze forced up to meet his.

"You'd better lock yourselves in tonight," he said. "I'll get back as early as I can tomorrow, and I'll bring a detective with me. Don't mention that. I won't announce that he's a detective. Just a new prospective foreman. George knows I suspect his loyalty now, though he denies having gone to the hangar last night. He swears he only started out in that direction, then turned off on another road."

"Do you think he might be the one who—"

"No—it's all crazy. But I'll do more checking. I'll recheck Enid's references too. Just take care, honey. Keep Bonnie with you, and don't take any chances while I'm away. I'll hurry back."

She thought she was prepared when she saw his mouth descending to hers. But there had never been anything in her life like the touch of his firm warm lips on hers, warmth that struck deeply through her whole being and seared like a flame. Without meaning to, she found herself responding fiercely.

After a brief, throbbing moment, he drew back to gaze down at her again. With a soft moan he held her tighter and pressed his cheek to hers.

"You're sweet, Anise. Be very careful while I'm gone. Nothing must happen to you!"

After he left she stood gazing at the closed door for a long time, waiting for her heartbeats to settle down to their normal rhythm.

"You're sweet," he had said. Did that mean he was falling in love with her? But what about Melanie? Would he even do something about Melanie so they could be together? In her sad condition, Melanie couldn't be much of a wife for any man. Couldn't he see to her care just as well, even if they weren't bound in marriage? Clay was sure she would be better off in a sanitarium under the care of psychiatrists.

Anise hoped something could be done—something he would consider honorable and wise—to release him even while he continued to fulfill his obligations. For there was no doubt in her own mind now. She couldn't fight it any longer. She loved him as she had never loved anyone else before in her life.

She had just started getting ready for bed when she heard the airplane zoom off into the distance. Fear settled down on her like a smothering blanket. Without his presence the whole household seemed rife with menace. There was no one else here she could trust, except maybe Clay. And now that her heart was so sure of her love for Greg, she wanted no more of Clay's light romancing.

Suddenly she wished she had gone with Greg. Why hadn't she insisted on his taking her and Bonnie with him on this trip so they would be safe? Did he actually believe there was no danger to them during his absence? How could he be sure?

She slept fitfully all night long. Every time strange noises awakened her, she wished again she and Bonnie had gone with Greg. But it was too late for that now. She tried to close her ears to the eerie wailing that came from Melanie's quarters, punctuated at times by the crash and clang of the old dumbwaiter. Once the wailing seemed to be centered just below her open window, then Anise realized that it was the puppy's howling she heard. Soon Carl's gutteral voice was calling softly, "Here Lady—come on, baby!" The wild yelping sounded joyful then as boy and dog were reunited.

By morning Anise was exhausted. Just a few hours to live through before Greg comes home, she told herself as she tried to wash the sleep from her eyes with cold water.

She found Bonnie awake but still in bed. "Did Daddy fly away again last night?" she asked. "I heard the plane once. When will he come back?"

"Sometime today, I hope. Meanwhile we'll say right together, every minute."

After breakfast she accompanied Bonnie for the tutoring session. Laura urged them to stay afterward and play games, but Bonnie declined emphatically. On their way back to their rooms she said, "Let's go for a little walk, Miss Weston. It's stuffy sticking around here, and so nice outside."

Anise hesitated. The early morning fog had cleared, leaving the sun bright on a sparkling blue sea. Would it be safe out there? Or was there less danger in their rooms?

Deirdre was in Bonnie's room, dusting the furniture. "Just cleaning up a bit," she said, as if she felt it necessary to offer an excuse for her presence.

"Shall we keep out of your way?" Anise asked. "We're thinking of taking a walk. It's too nice to stay inside."

"I'll say!" Deirdre smiled. The hostility, that had cloaked her since Clay's invitation to fly Anise to a dance, seemed now to have vanished. Clay must have done a good job of soothing her feelings night before last, Anise thought idly.

"I'll tell you what," Deirdre said. "I'm through cleaning up at this place. How'd you like to walk up to the cottage with me to see what needs to be done up there? With me along you won't be so likely to get lost. Or—or . . . well, Mr. Gregory said I was to keep close watch over you two."

Then Greg must feel they would be safe with Deirdre, Anise decided as they agreed to go with her. Yet when they were alone with the girl on the secluded woodsy trail to the cabin, she wondered how Greg could be sure that Deirdre wasn't the source of the menace. She immediately scoffed at the idea. Deirdre seemed as normal as anyone at Mendolair, and it would take someone completely off-balance to try to do away with Anise simply because she was a threat to her romance with Clay. There seemed no possible reason for her wanting Bonnie out of the way.

149

I'm spooking at shadows if I think Deirdre poses any danger, she told herself, and breathed easier.

As they came out of the woods into the clearing where the cottage was in view, the puppy came bounding to meet them. Carl was in the kitchen, grumbling to himself as he sloppily mopped the linoleum floor.

"Bart's supposed to be helping me," he told Deirdre, "but he went shooting and made me stay here."

"He went shooting?" Deirdre asked sharply. "Where?"

Carl shrugged. "At the range, I guess. He wouldn't let me go."

"You stay here," Deirdre said, "and keep Lady with you. I'll be back soon to help with your work."

She turned to Anise. "You and Bonnie come with me. Let's see what's going on. I know a place where we can't be seen."

She led them to the trail toward the ridge which Anise and Bonnie had followed after they were attacked by Mancho.

"We were shot at one day along here," Anise protested. This could be a trap to put them in danger. Could Deirdre be conniving in some scheme of Bart's to make them targets for more gunfire?

"The shooting won't be here today," Deirdre said. "You can hear it now, over on the range beyond that cliff."

Anise listened, and heard the shots, but they weren't loud.

"I'm scared," Bonnie said, clinging to her hand.

"There's nothing to be scared of here," Deirdre insisted. "We'll be in the woods in a minute where no one can see us."

She didn't take the trail leading upward over the ridge, but followed a lower one that led off to the side. Just as she promised, they were soon in deep woods, following a switchback trail that led uphill through the forest. They emerged at the top of a bluff.

"Get down on your knees now so the bushes will hide us," Deirdre said, kneeling to peer over the drop-off. Keeping Bonnie close, Anise inched up beside her, alert to any sudden move Deirdre might make. It would be disaster if the woman managed to push them over the edge of the cliff.

That was impressed on her even more keenly as she stared down to the steep rocky gorge below. The drop was so sheer that the base of the bluff was out of sight beneath them. The long flat gully was ideal for rifle practice, muffling the sound, as well as providing a backdrop at one end where targets were set up.

She identified Bart promptly, but it took a moment or two for her to realize that it was Miss Enid whom he was showing how to adjust the rifle at her shoulder and sight along the barrel. Why on earth would he be giving *her* lessons?

"Does Gregory know about this?" she asked sharply.

"How do I know?" Deirdre replied with a shrug. "I didn't know about it myself until just now."

"But you suspected something, didn't you? Isn't that why you brought us up here to see?"

"No . . . not exactly. I knew Bart spent a lot of time here and I got the idea that he didn't come alone. Look! There's Laura!"

The child had run out from the base of the cliff where she had been out of sight. She reached for the rifle, virtually took it away from her teacher, and turned to Bart. It was obvious that she was demanding instruction too, and Bart promptly obliged.

"Why would he teach a little girl to shoot a gun?" Deirdre asked in a tone of disgust. "She's hardly big enough to handle the darn thing. But I know she was always talking about going hunting with Bart someday. And that kid gets about anything she wants around here. No wonder she's spoiled."

"If they're only practicing to go hunting," Anise said, feeling sick, "why have they made such a secret of it?"

"Maybe it isn't really a secret," Deirdre pointed out. "Maybe we're the only ones who didn't know. Or maybe they just started. From the way both Laura and Miss Enid handle that gun I bet they couldn't hit the side of the house."

"Just the same, I don't want them shooting at us. Let's get out of here before they see us."

As they walked back to the cottage she resolved to see that Greg was informed about this as soon as he got home. Meanwhile she and Bonnie would wait until Deirdre was through at the cottage and ready to walk back to the house. She didn't want to be alone with Bonnie if they met those hunters in the woods!

CHAPTER 15

Anise awoke after a restless night to find the room dim, the window blanked with heavy, dripping fog. It added to the sense of fear and depression she had felt since last night when the day had passed without Greg's return. They had been socked in with fog since midafternoon, and it must have persisted all night. She was sure Greg hadn't flown in, for if she had slept at all, her sleep was so light the sound of the plane or jeep would surely have awakened her.

When the first gong sounded she got up and went to see if Bonnie were awake. The child was sitting up in bed.

"Did my Daddy come home?" she asked worriedly.

"I didn't hear the plane, did you?"

Bonnie shook her head. "Let's go down to breakfast and see. I'm tired of eating in your room."

Anise had asked for lunch and dinner to be served here yesterday because she felt safer. Yet there wasn't any real security here either, unless she locked the doors. They couldn't keep themselves prisoners indefinitely. Besides, it worried Bonnie.

So, much as she dreaded meeting the rest of the household with this new knowledge about the target range on her mind, she supposed they had better go down to breakfast.

Maybe it would calm her uneasiness if she casually asked

152

Bart, or Enid and Laura, about the shooting lessons. If they reacted normally, as if they had never meant to keep them a secret, perhaps she would feel less concern. After all, with so many people interested in hunting in an area like this, it could be quite natural for a ten-year-old girl and her governess to be interested, too.

Clay and Bart, Enid and Laura were already seated at the breakfast table when Anise took Bonnie downstairs. Both men promptly got up to seat them.

"We missed you at dinner last night," Clay said, smiling. "With Greg gone too, it was a pretty dull meal."

"We were tired," Anise said lamely.

"We went walking yesterday," Bonnie said, speaking directly to Bart. "We looked down from a cliff and saw you showing Miss Enid and Laura how to shoot."

"You did?" Bart looked surprised, but not alarmed. "Where were you? Why didn't you come on down and join us?"

Bonnie shuddered. "I don't like guns. They kill things."

Bart laughed. "I'm afraid you'll never make a hunter, if that's how you feel. One of these days I'm going to take Enid and Laura hunting, and if they bag something I bet you'll be glad enough to eat roast duck or fried rabbit."

"Not if they kill it!" Bonnie protested. Bart laughed again.

"You wouldn't want to eat it alive, would you?" he chided.

Breakfast was scarcely over when Deirdre rushed in, pale and distraught.

"We've got to find Melanie!" she cried. "She must have got out sometime during the night wearing nothing but a nightie and that flimsy thing she calls a peignoir. Somebody unlocked her door! No telling where she is by now! She'll catch her death out in this fog!"

"Where are George and Fannie?" Clay asked as both men got to their feet.

"They've already gone to look for her. They said we've all got to help. It's going to be hard to spot her in the fog if she's trying to hide. Mom went toward the cottage, Dad took the jeep up the hangar road and he'll search the woods on that side."

"All right," Clay said, immediately taking charge. "We'll divide up the other possibilities. Anise, you and Bonnie follow the path you're familiar with past the quarry road. Don't go up to the quarry—not under any circumstances. I'll take care

153

of that area. If you don't find her by the time you get to the beach, come on back and report. If you do find her, keep her in sight, but don't try to control her by yourself. I'll give you a whistle to blow. One that can be heard far enough for some of us to come and help you."

He turned to Bart and started lining out the area he should cover, while Miss Enid and Laura waited for their instructions.

Anise took Bonnie up to their rooms. She felt more like locking their doors and staying right there. But she could hardly refuse to help in an emergency like this when every possible person was needed to cover the area.

She dressed Bonnie in a hooded jacket and warm slacks. She wore her heaviest sweater for protection against the drizzly fog. Even so, she found herself shivering as they searched carefully through the garden, checking out all the branching paths.

They could scarcely see the bright colors of the flowers in the deep gloom. Deirdre was right, Anise reflected. It was like the old needle-in-the-haystack cliché, hunting for Melanie in fog like this.

There was no sign of her around the shed housing the generator, or along the chainlink fence encircling the reservoir. As they walked along the well-marked trail through the woods, Anise called Melanie's name softly, expecting no response. She could hear other voices in the distance, calling more loudly. But if Melanie had deliberately slipped away, she probably wouldn't answer.

Who had unlocked her door, allowing her to escape? Was it Deirdre's carelessness again? Or was someone deliberately letting the woman run into danger? With the delusions that plagued her, there was no telling where she might go, or what she would do. Surely if she became cold and wet in the drippy mist, she would have the sense to go back to the house. Provided, of course, that she could find it.

On their way through the woods Anise heard a snapping sound, as if someone were following them. She caught Bonnie's hand and warned her to silence as they paused and listened. The sound wasn't repeated. The birds were silent. Nothing but the bleating of a foghorn and the distant wailing of Melanie's name could be heard. No one appeared, so they walked on.

Crossing the meadow, she kept looking back, but a follower

could remain less than fifty feet back and be hidden behind the blank wall of the fog.

Zero visibility, she thought as she plodded on, her heart thundering in her ears, her hand clutching Bonnie's hand tight until the child protested, "You're squeezing too hard!"

"Sorry," Anise murmured. She couldn't banish the fear that bore down on her like haunting figures looming from the heavy mist. She tried to remember how the meadow looked in bright sunlight, with wild flowers blooming in the green grass and cattle browsing along the meandering stream.

Suddenly she thought she saw something move out toward the ocean cliffs where fog seemed to be thinning a little. Thinking it might be a cow coming toward them, Anise grabbed Bonnie's hand and paused, ready for flight.

"What is it?" Bonnie whispered, peering in the same direction.

It wasn't a cow, Anise realized as a faint silhouette emerged, like a tall and slender apparition taking form and floating toward them. It could be someone else hunting Melanie. . . .

Clutching Bonnie's hand tighter, Anise moved toward the dim figure. It was approaching faster now, faint green outlines growing more distinct. . . .

"It's Melanie!" she gasped. Melanie in the filmy green peignoir Deirdre said she was wearing.

As they came face to face, Melanie saw them too and stopped abruptly, her hand at her throat. For a startled moment they stared at each other while Anise considered frantically what to say to the woman to calm the terror that twisted her features.

"Sylvia!" Melanie gasped with a broken cry as she whirled about and ran back into the mist, her long wet skirts flapping, wild hair flying.

"Wait, Melanie, wait!" Anise cried as she plunged after the disappearing figure, aware of Bonnie running beside her.

"Wait—I'm not Sylvia!" she shouted, but Melanie gave no indication that she heard.

Remembering the whistle Clay had given her with instructions not to try to control Melanie by herself, she took it from her pocket and blew on it frantically, at the same time trying to keep Melanie in view.

Alternately calling and blowing the whistle, she ran on, stumbling sometimes on the uneven ground. Once Bonnie fell down, and Anise waited breathlessly to help her up, then they both rushed on, trying to catch up.

It was like running endlessly on a ghostly plateau somewhere out in space, surrounded by a wall of mist, following a phantom figure that was in sight one minute, lost the next, emerging into view again as the mists shifted about.

At a moment when Melanie was clearly visible against the pearly mist, she suddenly disappeared, dropping completely out of sight. Her thin scream of terror seemed to come up to them out of a void.

"The cliff!" Anise cried, grabbing Bonnie, holding her tight, trembling violently with horror that deepened as Melanie's frantic shrieks continued.

"Bonnie, be careful!" Anise quavered. "Don't go any closer! She fell over the cliff!"

Hearing the sound of running water nearby, she realized this was the slippery spot where Greg had warned her the stream cascaded over rocks into the deep cove below—one of the most dangerous and rocky coves along the coast.

She blew the whistle again, as loud as she could, still holding Bonnie close.

"Let's move carefully now," she cautioned, "And maybe we can get close to the edge and talk to her until help comes."

Still blowing the whistle, she held Bonnie's hand as they inched their way toward the bluff, kneeling down to crawl the last few feet when the brink was in sight.

"Melanie, listen!" she called trying to peer over. Melanie's wailing continued, as if she had no awareness of anything beyond her own pain and terror. Anise couldn't see her among the jumble of jagged wet rocks far below. There was no beach, only the rocky cove partly inundated by the crashing breakers.

Help must come soon, she thought fearfully. And whoever came had better bring a rope. Otherwise they could never bring Melanie up the steep pitch of this inward-curving, overhanging cliff. The woman was probably too confused and frightened to be able to hang on to a rope by herself, or even to tie it around her waist. Someone would have to be lowered to help her, and they had better bring the truck to secure the rope from above and pull them out. . . .

"Hang on tight, Melanie," she called down into the gloom. The mist didn't seem as thick down near the water, yet Melanie was still out of sight. Her wails were subsiding into hopeless

156

whimpers, and Bonnie was trying to comfort her too, kneeling beside Anise to peer over the edge.

At last, with a great sense of relief, Anise heard running footsteps behind them and knew that help had finally arrived.

"Watch out for the cliff!" she warned, starting to get to her feet. She was still not solidly balanced when she half turned and saw that it was only Miss Enid and Laura. They wouldn't be any help at all!

At the same moment, with a feeling of complete incredulity, she saw the frenzied intentness of Enid's expression, eyes crazed, mouth stretched wide to bare her crooked teeth as she lunged straight toward her, giving her shoulder a violent shove.

"No! . . . Unable to catch her balance, or grab for anything but thin air, she felt a scream tear at her throat as the frightful sensation of falling possessed her like a nightmare.

Still grabbing wildly, her hand closed on something—a scratchy growth of some kind. It nearly jerked her arm from its socket, but it stopped her fall, and swung her inward where she could get a meager foothold in some sort of niche in the side of the cliff.

At the same instant she heard Bonnie's scream and saw the small body go hurtling past, down to the misty darkness below where her scream ended in abrupt and ominous silence.

Oh Bonnie, Bonnie. . . . Dear God, it must have killed her! Anise felt herself sobbing without making a sound. Her breath was caught on pain that choked her. She had failed the child after all. She hadn't protected her carefully enough—or cleverly enough.

"We won't need these guns now." Miss Enid's voice was low and harsh, sounding just above, barely audible against the roar of the sea. "I can't see them down there, but with the tide this high and still coming in, they couldn't possibly get out of there alive. No one will ever know what happened. It's better than shooting, so I hope you're satisfied."

Anise couldn't mark their departure, but the silence lasted so long she was sure they were gone. Meanwhile the rocky niche was slippery and her hand was growing weak on the plant she was clutching. Also, it seemed to be pulling loose from the crevice where it had somehow taken root. She tried to examine the cliff extending below her, saw a ledge where

157

she might hope to get enough footing to spring over to a larger projection beyond.

She had to make the attempt, for she couldn't hang on here much longer. Besides, she must get down there to see if she could find Bonnie. Praying that the child might be miraculously still alive, she swung one leg for as much momentum as possible, and aimed herself at the ledge, straining every muscle with the effort. She landed skidding, grabbing wildly, then the momentum carried her on to the projecting rock. It was slippery too, and for a moment she thought she could never hold on. But a rough protrusion gave her a handhold, and her feet found something solid.

The mist was clearing a little now. She glanced about wildly for a sight of Bonnie's still form somewhere, but there was nothing but rocks and water. Was the child submerged in one of the swirling pools left from the backwash of a breaker?

Melanie continued to wail and whimper, but the sound had grown weaker and was audible only during the brief space of time when each wave was sucked back toward the ocean to prepare for the next breaker. Melanie's voice seemed to come from the other side of the cove, near the waterfall that splashed down over the rocks. She must have skidded into the gully and the waterfall washed her in that direction.

"Miss Weston!"

It was Bonnie's weak voice calling faintly from somewhere just below.

"Oh thank God! She's alive!" Murmuring fervent prayers of relief, Anise scrambled down the rock toward the sound. Sharp edges scraped her flesh already cut and scratched from her fall. She finally lost hold and dropped into rolling water that swept her up onto a fairly flat rock where she lay panting for a moment, trying to catch her breath.

Bonnie was huddled in a shallow cave, standing waist deep in the foam of a receding wave. Apparently the child had fallen into water, too, rather than onto rocks that could have killed her.

"I'm hiding," Bonnie said tremulously. "I'm afraid they might throw rocks down on us, or shoot us. Now I *know* Laura hates me! She pushed me!"

"I know, darling. Are you all right?" In the dim, misty shadows of the cave it was hard to tell. At least she was on her feet.

"I'm bumped all over and bleeding, and it hurts," Bonnie complained. "I fell clear under the water, too, but I did like Daddy showed me how to dead-man's float, and I didn't get water up my nose."

"Good for you!" Anise declared thankfully. That swimming lesson probably saved her life.

"But I'm scared," Bonnie went on. "It's wet and cold down here. How can we get out?"

Anise didn't know how to answer. Enid had sounded positive when she said that with the high tide still rising they couldn't possibly get out alive. But there must be a way!

"Can you get over to this rock?" Anise asked. "We'll look for Melanie, then see if we can find a way for us all to climb out."

"I'm afraid they'll see us!" Bonnie quavered. "What if they're not gone yet? Laura has a gun. She pushed me with it. They could shoot us!"

Anise stared upward. The fog was clearing enough to show the ragged edge of the bluff against the misty sky. She could see, too, with a sinking heart, how impossible that bluff would be to climb, the precipitous vertical wall inclining inward toward a series of caves at the base. Caves that would soon be underwater, she realized as a fresh wave roared in. Steep cliffs also flanked the cove at each side, out to the rocky promontories where waves were crashing high with the incoming tide.

"I'm pretty sure there's no one up there now," she told Bonnie. "Let's see if we can find Melanie."

They climbed over a jumble of rocks and sand, and found Melanie on the other side, in water up to her shoulders as a wave foamed over her. Her tangled hair was soaked with brine. There was a dark bruise over one eye and on her cheek below it.

"I can't get up!" she wailed. "I thing my leg is broken."

"We'll help you. Give me your hand." As the wave receded Anise stepped down beside the woman and tried to assist her to her feet. But one leg was swollen and bleeding, broken to an angle that left bone protruding from tattered flesh.

She shouldn't be moved, Anise thought in panic. But if they left her here she would drown. The next moment that became terrifyingly certain as a new wave washed completely over her, burying her in crashing foam.

159

Melanie came up gasping and gagging as the wave receded. They had to get her out of this hollow.

"Bonnie, see if you can hold her leg in both arms and keep it steady while I try to drag her up on this rock. Melanie, you can help too. Hang on to me, and try to push with your good leg."

It seemed an endless struggle, with Melanie screaming in pain at every move. They lost ground each time a new wave crashed in, almost dislodging them from the jumble of rocks they were climbing. But finally they worked their way to the heightest point above water on the floor of the cove. They would have to be rescued before the tide rose above their perch, or Miss Enid's prediction would come true.

Anise saw Bonnie staring around the rocky walls surrounding them, in clearer view now as the mist continued to thin.

"We can't get out, can we?" the child murmured, looking faint with dismay. "If the water gets too high, we'll drown!" She buried her face in trembling hands.

"Maybe help will come before then, Bonnie. I'll blow the whistle and—"

"No! They'll hear us and come back with their guns!" Bonnie sounded more terrified of that than of the water. And she was right, of course. Enid and Laura might not be far away. On the other hand, they might have been anxious to put as much distance as possible between them and their wicked deed.

"We have to have help, Bonnie. Maybe the Mortons, or Clay, or someone else who likes us will hear the whistle and come to help."

She reached into her pocket, but the whistle wasn't there. She must have had it in her hand when Enid pushed her. No telling where it had landed.

Melanie had fallen silent, seemingly in deep shock from the pain and struggle of moving her broken leg. Her face was deathly white except for the dark bruises. Anise reached over to take her pulse, to be sure she was still alive.

Melanie opened her eyes and stared at her, looking bewildered. "You're not Sylvia, are you? I keep thinking you are, then I know you aren't. I guess I've been confused. I can't seem to remember things."

"Sylvia's dead," Anise told her.

"I know, but she keeps coming back to get revenge. If she's

160

dead, she knows everything now, doesn't she? She knows I lied to her about Greg, and she'll find a way to punish me."

"You lied about Greg?" Anise asked sharply.

Melanie began to cry. "She always got the best of everything," she sobbed. "She got Greg. All I got was a cheap affair with Clay!"

"You're Greg's wife," Anise reminded her. "But you were engaged to Clay once, weren't you?"

Melanie stopped crying and turned to her. "How did you know?"

"Clay told me."

The woman's eyes narrowed, the bruised and swollen one closing completely. Her mouth twisted as if in sudden agony. "Did Clay tell you he's Laura's father? Did he tell you that?"

"No!" Anise pressed her hand to her throat where her heart seemed to have leaped up to thump painfully. So that's why Greg was leaving the bulk of his estate to Bonnie. She was actually the only direct heir! But why hadn't he told her?

"Nobody was supposed to know," Melanie moaned, turning her face away, beginning to talk fast and urgently as if she had to relieve herself of some terrible burden. "Sylvia wouldn't trust Greg and it made him mad. He was mad at Clay too. Clay was always having to be bailed out of trouble. Greg would have made him marry me, but Clay had shipped off to South America and we couldn't find him. So Greg married me to give Laura her father's name."

She began to laugh, but the laughter quickly changed to tearful sobbing. Anise stared at her. Had she been telling the truth? Or was this more of her insane babbling?

Melanie stopped crying and stared at her again. "You think I'm crazy, don't you? I guess I am, sometimes. That's what they tell me when I can't keep track of things. But I'm not crazy now. Oh, I know we're going to die. I don't even care anymore. Greg will never love me."

"I'm sure he does!" Anise protested, remembering his tenderness the afternoon she had seen them together. "You're his wife!"

Melanie's mouth twisted, and bitterness was reflected in her eyes. "That's what *you* think! He treats me like a child! I could be Laura for all he. . . . Sometimes I hate him!"

She bared her teeth in a grin. "But you can't have him, either! We'll all die here!" Again she laughed hysterically, the

161

sound merging into a wail of pain as she tried to adjust her fractured leg.

For what seemed hours they shivered in their wet clothes, watching the water rise as the waves crashed higher. Perhaps it wasn't as long as it seemed, Anise thought, but her watch had been smashed in her fall, and she lost track of time. The mist was clearing faster, and patches of blue sky became visible above. But what good would that do, if no one found them in time?

Melanie continued to babble, sometimes rationally, at other times completely unintelligibly. Wet and bedraggled in the clinging peignoir, shivering with pain and fear, she was a pathetic sight. Anise could feel nothing but compassion for the woman, in spite of the havoc she had wrought in several lives. Without her malicious lie to destroy Sylvia's faith, Greg and Sylvia might have remained happily married.

On the other hand, Anise mused, if Sylvia's faith in Greg was so weak that, instead of trusting her husband, she believed an envious woman's lie bolstered only by unproven circumstancial evidence, perhaps the marriage was doomed to failure anyway.

Anise surmised, from Melanie's hysterical rambling, that it may have been her burdening sense of guilt, coupled with the disappointment of unrequited love, that had unbalanced her mind.

When a wave larger than ever rushed over them, almost dislodging them from the mound of rocks where they perched precariously, Anise knew they must find a higher place of refuge or they would soon be washed out to sea.

"Look, Bonnie," she said, pointing to a rocky ledge at one side of the cove. "As soon as this next wave is past, let's climb around to that little shelf over there before another breaker crashes in. That spot is higher than this, and we may be able to hang on until help comes."

She turned to Melanie, gravely doubtful as she asked, "Do you think you could make it? We've got to do something! We'll help you all we can. Try to stand up so we can get a quick start when the next wave recedes. We won't have much time between waves. Come on, give me your hand."

They might get caught in one or two breakers on the way, she thought. But if the current didn't prove too strong in either the wave or the backflow, they should be able to weather them. It might be less painful for Melanie in the water, than trying to drag that broken leg over the rocks.

"What's the use?" Melanie grumbled. "You know darn well nobody's coming to help us." But she obediently struggled to her good foot, and, the three of them stood holding hands, bracing themselves as one more comber crashed against the rocks and came roaring in to drench them along with their perch. At the height of the breaker Bonnie was in swirling water almost up to her neck. She lost her footing under the force of the backwash.

Anise let go of Melanie's hand in order to grab the child. She managed, with difficulty, to keep her own footing and hold Bonnie. But she could do nothing about it when Melanie gave one last percing scream and plunged into the receding wave, immediately lost to sight in the swirling foam.

It looked almost as if she had flung herself down deliberately. As if she'd had all the pain and terror she could endure. Anise had not time to think about it now. Holding Bonnie's hand tight, she guided her down the jumble of rocks, over what appeared to be the most negotiable course around and across the cove to the ledge.

They didn't quite beat the next breaker, but there was a sharp, upward thrust of rock to which they could cling while the water foamed around them. Then they pushed on, stumbling, skidding, sliding, until they made their way to the far side of the cove, gained foothold on a few protruding rocks, and struggled up to a small shelf where they could sit securely, safe from the rising water for a little while longer.

CHAPTER 16

For another untimed period they sat huddled in the narrow niche, watching the water rise, counting the waves. For about five breakers, each would crash higher, then there would be a series of smaller ones. Each time hope was born that the tide had started to ebb, the waves would become larger again, and five more would bring the peak to a higher level than ever. She knew from high water marks visible now in pale sunlight, that it was likely to rise many feet above their perch.

Glancing down at Bonnie, who had grown quiet, she saw the child's small hands clasped below her chin while she murmured words that were inaudible under the roar of the ocean and the squawking of seagulls. After a moment Bonnie looked up smiling.

"I was saying my prayers," she said. "Now I'm sure God will get us out of here."

Anise felt tears sting her eyes. Bonnie has more courage and faith than I have, she thought with a pang of guilt. Maybe I should pray, too, or—more to the point right now—I'd better see if I can possibly find a way to help God answer her prayer.

"You stay here, Bonnie," she said firmly, moving out of the way so she could wedge Bonnie's small form as far back into the niche as possible. "Now that sunshine is making everything

164

visible, I'm going to look around and see if I can get a better view of the walls of this cove and find a way to climb out."

She knew it was dangerous, because she had to scramble down almost to the floor of the cove between waves. If a large breaker caught her, she could be washed out to sea as Melanie had been.

Clinging to rough projections, with her feet still on the narrow ledge, she worked her way toward the promontory. The little shelf led downward, and to her horror, the most tremendous wave yet came crashing in, it's swirling foam rushing toward her.

She tightened her hands on the sharp edge of a projecting rock and leaned hard against the cliff as the wave foamed past, splashing almost to her waist. When the water receded she began to feel secure again. Then, without warning, the ledge crumbled beneath her feet, and her fingers couldn't hold her weight.

She found herself sliding, grabbing wildly for anything she could find. Sharp edges tore at her flesh as she slid on down into the rushing water.

When it seemed that nothing would save her from being washed out to sea, she came up hard against the side of a sharply pointed rock and clung to it with all her might, while the wave continued to recede, finally leaving her above water.

Glancing upward, she saw Bonnie waving frantically from the niche. The child's mouth was moving, but the words were lost in the roar of the rushing backwash.

She didn't really hear the plane, yet in the quiet moment between waves, there seemed to be a continuation of sound that didn't come from the ocean. She glanced up and saw the familiar small aircraft coming into view above the far side of the cove.

"Gregory! Greg!" she screamed, even though she knew he couldn't hear her. She climbed as high as she could on the rock and waved. She pulled off her sweater and swung it around, yelling at the top of her voice.

The wings tilted slightly. Did Greg see her?

But then he flew on, and she slumped back down to the rock. If he hadn't seen her, there was no hope of rescue. From this point she could spot no possible way of climbing over the promontory. The cliff above the niche where Bonnie was wedged was just as unscalable.

A new wave was coming, so all she could do was cling to the rock and let it wash over her. She had no time to put her sweater back on, and she was unable to hang on to it in the force of the wave that swept past. If the next wave came in any stronger, she wasn't sure she could hang on at all.

She wondered if she could make her way back to Bonnie. While she was studying the possibility, the next wave crashed in. It took all her strength to cling to the rock. But she had seen a way back to the ledge, if only she could hurry fast enough to beat the next breaker.

Shivering in her drenched clothes, bleeding, hurting all over from cuts and bruises, she struggled through the receding water, back toward the spot where they had climbed to the ledge in the first place. Her fingers were almost too numb to hold on now, her feet felt like stumps, and her drenched clothes, rough with sand and salt, stuck painfully to her skin. Yet somehow, sobbing with near panic, she made her way back to the niche.

At least we're together, whatever happens, she thought, holding Bonnie close in trembling arms.

"I saw Daddy's plane!" Bonnie shouted above the roar of another breaker. "Do you think he saw us?"

"I hope so, Bonnie! We'll pray that he did."

It seemed a long time, and many waves later before the jeep could be heard during a lull between waves.

"He came!" Bonnie shouted. Anise was too weak and shaky with relief to make a sound. Holding Bonnie tight so the child wouldn't fall in her excitement, she gazed up along the top of the cliff.

He came into view first above the back wall, glancing about searchingly.

"Here! We're over here!" She tried to shout, but her voice was only a weak tremor. Bonnie was yelling, however, and her high treble voice must have carried, for he saw them and waved. Immediately he disappeared, and a moment later he was right above them, lowering a rope.

"There's a loop in the end of this," he shouted. "Slip it around Bonnie's waist and tell her to hold on tight. Then we'll send it back to you."

Her hands were almost too numb to handle the rope, but Bonnie helped to secure herself in the loop. When the rope came back for Anise, it was all she could do to sit in the loop and hang on. At the top she collapsed in Gregory's arms, and to her chagrin, began to sob.

"There, there . . ." he crooned, patting her shoulder. "It's all over now. You're safe and sound."

She couldn't stop crying. "Melanie drowned," she sobbed against his shoulder. "And I almost let Bonnie die. I was so stupid—I let them push us over the cliff!"

"Who?" His body stiffened, his voice was harsh. "Who pushed you?"

When she told him, he grasped her by the shoulders and held her back to glare down at her. "You mean Laura—too? But she's just a child! That woman's responsible! Enid! She's been a terrible influence on the poor kid! I don't know how I could have been so mistaken in hiring her! She's a drug addict! I found that out in my investigation. I was hurrying home to fire her!"

She gazed at him appalled. Even in the face of this evidence, he wasn't going to believe his precious Laura was malicious. She wiped tears from her eyes and wondered how she could convince him. Until she did, Bonnie would never be safe.

"Where is everybody?" he asked. "There was no one at the house when we drove past."

She told him about the search for Melanie, noting meanwhile that a stranger was standing behind the jeep. Presently Greg introduced him as Jim Kramer, a private detective.

"I engaged him to help with Enid's investigation, and to come here to see what he could make out of all that's going on. He can take Enid back with him when he goes. Let's drive to the house now so you and Bonnie can get into dry clothes. Your teeth are chattering."

He put Bonnie in the back seat, asked Mr. Kramer to drive, then helped Anise in and got in beside her. Bonnie curled up in his lap and fell into an exhausted sleep. Anise snuggled close in the curve of his arm, feeling warm and safe at last.

"I don't think Enid's the main threat to Bonnie's life," Anise said gravely as they drove across the meadow. "Because I can't believe Laura's innocent. There are lots of things that don't make sense. Clay told me he was engaged to Melanie once, and you broke it up. You didn't deny it when I asked you. Before she died, Melanie told me that Laura is Clay's child. He

167

took off to South America, so you married her to give Laura his name, since it's the same as your own."

"That's true," he said quietly. "I didn't think Melanie was sane enough to. . . . Good Lord, I hope she hasn't told Laura! I didn't want Laura to know until she and Clay had established such a good relationship she would welcome him as her father. Also, until she matured enough to be tolerant of the circumstances and not let it affect her self-image."

Anise sighed with frustration. "Melanie seemed quite sane at times while we were stranded in the cove, Greg. When she was sure I wasn't Sylvia, she expressed the fear that Sylvia knows everything now that she's gone beyond this life. She thought Sylvia was somehow punishing her for the lie she told to break up your marriage."

"The lie?" Greg was frowning at her.

Anise nodded. "The Dimmicks told me about it too. While Sylvia was in the hospital with Bonnie, Melanie told her she was going to have your baby. Apparently there was other evidence of an affair, neighbors told her Melanie had been hanging around your house. Before Sylvia could question you about it, she found you holding Melanie in your arms, and she blew up."

He was silent for a long moment, scowling at the back of Kramer's head as they bounced over the rough road. Finally he drew a deep breath. "That's why she wouldn't believe me, no matter what I said. And I was too angry at her lack of faith to try very hard to make her understand. So she rushed to Reno for a divorce, and hated me ever after."

As Mr. Kramer stopped the jeep in front of the house, Greg's arm tightened about Anise. "I want you to know I'm sorry about putting you in such danger here. I had no idea anything like this would happen. But just the same," his smile was bleak, "I can't help being glad you're here. You're still miraculously alive, and you saved Bonnie."

He stepped out with Bonnie hoisted over his shoulder still half asleep. Anise needed the hand he offered to steady her, for her knees were rubbery when she tried to stand.

They went into the house, but no one was there.

"Better get Bonnie bathed and put to bed," Greg told her. "And get into dry clothes yourself. Then come downstairs. We need to talk some more, preferably before the rest of the household shows up. I want you to go over everything careful-

168

ly with Mr. Kramer, and see what he makes of the situation."

Exhausted from her ordeal, Bonnie could hardly stay awake long enough for a warm bath, and some bandaging of the worst of her cuts. She snuggled under the covers and seemed to fall promptly to sleep.

Anise hurried through a shower to wash off the salt water and sand, then applied bandages to her own wounds. She dressed quickly, anxious to confer with Greg and the detective. As she started down the stairs, the two men came from the living room. Greg glanced up and saw her.

The whole family seems to be arriving at once," he said. "Stay out of sight in here until I call you. I want to hear what they have to say before they know you and Bonnie are safe."

She stood by the door, holding it open a crack.

"We thought we heard your plane come in," Mr. Morton's gruff voice announced. "But we kept on trying to find Melanie. Someone left her door open and she wandered off. Now we can't find Bonnie and Miss Weston either."

"Melanie is dead," Greg said quietly. Anise heard a chorus of concern as the group moved in closer to the porch. Their words were indistinct because several spoke at once.

"I know where Bonnie is," Greg said, then into the sudden silence he added, "She's upstairs in bed, and Miss Weston is right here at the door."

As she stepped out onto the porch, Anise watched Enid and Laura, saw their faces blanch with fright. Laura grabbed Enid's arm and glanced about wildly as if looking for someplace to run. Enid stood her ground, the fear in her face settling into grim defiance as she stared at Greg.

"What kind of cock and bull story did they tell you about where they've been?" Enid challenged.

"They didn't have to tell me where they'd been, for I found them there myself. Down in the cove, about to be drowned, as Melanie was. You and Laura shoved them over the cliff." He turned on Laura. "You deliberately tried to kill Bonnie! Why?"

For a moment Laura flinched, looking ready to dart in any direction that offered escape. Then, abruptly, she ran to Greg, sobbing, "She made me! I didn't want to hurt my sister! Miss Enid made me! She said she'd throw me to the sharks if I didn't! She pinched me! She beat me!"

"That's a lie!" Enid stepped forward, her face white, her

169

dun colored eyes glittering. "Your precious brat's a monster! She's the one doing all the dirty work around here! She turned Mancho loose at the cotage and then tried to shoot them. When she found she couldn't shoot straight she got Bart to give her lessons. Me, too. I'm afraid of guns but she made me—"

"How could a mere child make you do anything?" Greg broke in, holding Laura close as she clung to him.

"I told you she's a monster! She tried to drown Bonnie! She pushed her down the dumbwaiter shaft, and into the quarry, too. She admitted it, but I couldn't report it because— Well, she's been blackmailing me. She threatened to tell all sorts of wild tales about me if I wouldn't get rid of Bonnie and Anise."

Greg's face was grim as he stared down at the woman. "You mean she threatened to expose your drug addiction! Threatened to report your buying heroin from a pusher who meets you at the park?"

For a long moment Enid stood unbreathing, her face a white mask of panic. Then bright pink slowly suffused her cheeks and she drew a long shaky breath.

"She—she told you anyway! The little sneak! I should've known I couldn't trust her. I might as well tell you all the other things she's done. She—"

"Hold it!" Greg placed his hands firmly on Laura's shoulders and made her face him. "I want to hear Laura tell me about it. Why have you been trying to kill Bonnie?"

"It wasn't my idea!" Laura said tearfully. "Uncle Clay said I *had* to! He said you were going to give her Mendolair and everything you own! He said my mother and I and all our family would be out in the cold and I'd be put in an orphanage. So he bought me a gun and said to ask Bart—"

"I didn't know you planned to shoot anybody!" Bart exclaimed, walking over to the child, fist clenched as if he'd like to strike her. "You said you wanted to learn to go hunting!" He turned to Greg, his brow creased. "Honest, Greg, I never dreamed—"

"Okay, skip it!" Greg cut in, his incredulous gaze intent on Laura, as if he couldn't believe what he'd been hearing. His hands must have been painfully tight on her shoulders, Anise thought, for the child cringed, and pulled at his fingers.

"Why didn't you ask *me*?" he demanded. "Why did you let Uncle Clay feed you a lot of lies?"

"He doesn't lie!" Laura declared. *"You* do! You called

170

yourself my daddy, but you're not! Uncle Clay is my daddy. My mother said so too. And so did—"

She glanced up at Mrs. Morton who had stepped forward, wringing her hands, wrinkling her brow. "I should have told you when Melanie. . . . But I didn't think she was sane—I didn't think she knew what she was talking about. And the way Laura's been acting—I didn't know it was this bad. We knew something was terribly wrong with her, but we hid it from you. We were afraid you'd think there's something wrong with our whole family, what with Carl and Melanie. . . . I didn't want you to kick us all out, the way Clay said you would if you knew. . . ."

"Where *is* Clay?" Greg snapped, his hands dropping from Laura's shoulders as he glanced sharply about.

Everyone stared around, but Clay wasn't with them. Then, on the other side of the house, the jeep's motor could be heard roaring to a loud crescendo as gears clashed and the vehicle took off.

Clay had slipped away while accusations were flying, Anise reflected as they all ran around the corner of the house just in time to see the jeep disappear at a curve in the road to the hangar.

"Get the truck out," Greg told Mr. Morton. "Kramer and I will go after him. He'll have to take time to fuel the plane before he can leave. The tank's practically empty."

As Morton rushed off, Greg continued, "Mr. Kramer has authority to make an arrest. But what will the charges be? Conspiring with a child to commit murder?" He frowned down at Laura, still seeming incredulous.

"Don't be mad at me!" Laura begged with a new rush of tears. "I only did what my real daddy told me to!"

"Please don't be too hard on her," Mrs. Morton said, taking Laura's hand. "I can understand your not wanting her around anymore, now that you have your own little girl, and Laura's turned out to be so bad. But she's our kin. George and I will look after her. If Clay will let us."

"Clay will have nothing to say about it!" Greg's mouth tightened. "Legally she's my child, and Clay hasn't a—" He paused at the sound of the plane taking off.

"That crazy fool!" he exclaimed as the plane zoomed into sight and flew past over the house. "He must have taken off without checking the fuel gauge! He couldn't possibly have

171

had time to fill. . . ." He let the sentence dangle as the engine sputtered and died.

Anise watched, every muscle tense, as the plane circled back. Apparently Clay was trying to fly it like a glider, as Greg had done one day. But there was no wind, and he didn't aim for the cliffs to find an updraft. Besides, he hadn't enough altitude for leeway as he tried to head back toward the airstrip. He wasn't as skillfully as his brother, either, she realized as the small aircraft began to lose altitude fast.

"Oh no! Dear God, no!" she cried, as suddenly the plane nosedived straight toward the house.

"Bonnie's in there!" she cried, trying to not to stumble as she ran as fast as she could to the door.

"Wait!" Greg called after her. "Don't go in the house!"

She paid no attention. She rushed through the door just as the plane crashed into their wing of the building. There was a deafening roar of shattering walls and timbers, and a jolt that momentarily knocked her off her feet.

Stunned, she scrambled up the stairs on hands and knees. "Oh God, don't let it be Bonnie's room!" she sobbed. The creaking crashing sounds continued as if the whole house were about to collapse. It must have been only seconds, but it seemed frantic hours before she reached the top of the stairs, stumbled to her feet, and ran toward their rooms. Before she reached her door, she found her way blocked by huge fallen timbers. This whole wing of the house was rocking now, the walls and floor slanting crazily.

She tried to climb over the fallen timbers, but it seemed impossible. It would be quicker to run down to the back stairway —if only that's clear, she thought frantically.

Retracing her steps back down the stairs, she found the bannister had fallen away. Some of the steps had crumpled, and the entrance had crashed in a mass of glass and lumber. Holding her breath, she dropped from the middle of the stairs, down to the hall below, and ran to the back stairway. It was splitting too, with the force of rocking that still made the house shudder. She thought of the butane furnace, and the tank of fuel. If the line had broken, a spark could cause an explosion and fire at any moment.

As she struggled up the stairs she could hear Bonnie screaming. "Hold on, Bonnie! I'm coming!" she sobbed, but her bones felt like water, her leg muscles almost too numb to carry her up a stairway that seemed endless.

The upper hall was clear, and, though the floor tilted crazily, she ran down to Bonnie's room. The door wouldn't open.

"Unlock it, Bonnie!" she cried, twisting the knob.

"It isn't locked!" Bonnie sobbed, banging against the door. "But I can't get it open!"

It must be jammed because the house is out of shape, Anise thought, shoving with all her might. She heard a crash somewhere, then the door gave way and slammed down with her into the room, knocking her breathless.

"Bonnie!" she gasped, afraid the door had fallen on the child. But Bonnie was all right. She had scrambled out of the way in time.

"Get up, Miss Weston!" Bonnie cried, sounding terrified. "The ceiling's falling down!"

Anise got to her feet, grabbed Bonnie's hand, and rushed to the window just as beams gave way and let the ceiling down behind them to angle across the room, blocking their way to the door.

Holding hands, they rushed through the bathroom, only to stop short as a tremendous explosion rocked the house.

"Oh my God!" Anise moaned. The furnace must have blown up. Or the tank of butane. Or both. As the floor shuddered beneath her, she ran to the door. Just as she feared, it was jammed under a sagging beam, and she couldn't get it open.

She ran to the window, Bonnie right beside her. There was no one below, and she knew it would be too far to jump safely.

"Bonnie, stay over by the bed!" she ordered. "We've got to get the door open!" She thought she detected the roar of fire now, above the creaking, crashing sounds of the crumbling framework. The whole house would burn like kindling!

Picking up the maple boudoir chair, she ran to the door and swung the chair against it. The blow made no impression. Using the chair like a battering ram, she rushed against the door again. The jolt knocked her breathless.

There was a splintering sound as the door gave way. Then something heavy crashed down on her head, and she blacked out.

173

CHAPTER 17

She was running and running, but her legs dragged and she could make no progress. Fire swept past her one minute, waves crashed over her the next, and she was too weak to cry out.

Gradually she became aware of a pleasant fragrance, and a gentle voice talking beside her. The words didn't come through clearly, but they had a soothing, comforting sound. She tried hard to lift her heavy eyelids. When she finally succeeded, the nightmare vanished. She was in a bright sunny room banked with flowers. Greg was sitting by her bed, looking tenderly concerned.

"Anise, darling," he murmured, "are you going to wake up at last?"

For a moment her memory seemed a complete blank. Then, as it returned, she sat up so suddenly it made her head swim.

"Bonnie!" she gasped. "Where's Bonnie?"

"Bonnie's all right," he said, his hands gentle as he forced her back to the pillow. "You must be quiet. You've had a skull fracture and serious concussion. You were a brave girl to find Bonnie and stay with her until we could bring the extension ladder to get you both out the window. You've been unconscious for almost a week."

174

"Oh dear . . . " she whispered. She wanted to ask what had been happening during that week, but she seemed to have lost her voice in the weakness that possessed her. She was so tired she felt herself drifting helplessly back to sleep.

This time there were no nightmares. During the days and nights that followed, she found her strength returning.

Gregory was beside her bed for hours every day, and, as she recovered, he briefed her on all that had happened. After she and Bonnie were safely out of the house, he said, she had been brought to the hospital by helicopter.

"I phoned for one from the cottage," he explained. "Bonnie is at the cottage now with the Mortons. She's having a ball with Carl and his puppy."

"What about Laura?" she asked fearfully.

His smile was sad. "Laura's presently at Juvenile Hall, being studied by child psychologists. Eventually the Mortons will take her, if she makes enough progress. She's emotionally warped from a combination of hereditary and environmental influences, but there's a chance she can be straightened out. It's a job for experts, first, then for someone who loves her, as the Mortons do. George and Fannie feel that she belongs to them."

"What about her—her. . . . What about Clay?" she asked.

"He died in the crash. Just about the sort of crash he tried to arrange for us, so he could marry Melanie and get his hands on everything I own. I was foolish to trust him when he came back wanting to work at the mill and live with us. I should have suspected ulterior motives. I guess a man like that never changes. With Kramer's help, I've been finding evidence that he was responsible for the sabotage that caused our machinery breakdowns. Pure malice because I refused to share ownership with him. I'm giving Bart a chance to take on his job at the mill now."

"I'm glad," she said. "I've liked Bart—though at times I was afraid to trust *anybody*. What about Enid?"

"She's in a sanitarium for drug addicts. I think there's hope for rehabilitation. And Deirdre wants to be a nurse, so I'll finance her training. I can do that much for Melanie's cousin."

"It seems to me you've been doing a lot for Melanie's family," she said, reaching out for his hand. "And after the harm she did you and Sylvia!"

175

That's the kind of person he was, she reflected, hoping he was going to love her the way she loved him.

"You lost your house," she added. "Did it burn down completely?"

"It didn't burn down at all. There was a fire after the explosion, but we had plenty of water from the reservoir to fight the flames. The damage from the crash is too extensive for repair, though, considering its age. We'll replace it with a rambling, modern ranch-style house, complete with swimming pool, tennis courts, and stables for a few good horses. Would you like that?"

"Me?" she gasped. "You mean. . . ."

He laughed and caught both her hands to his lean cheeks. "That wasn't a very romantic proposal, was it? I hope you know by now that I love you. I want you with me always. And when you leave this bed so you can go with me to some beautiful spot along the shore—maybe that gazebo looking out over the ocean—I'm going to ask you that important question. I hope your answer will include setting an early wedding date. Bonnie and I need you, darling."

As he bent over, she wound her arms about his neck and met his lips with her own, eager and tremulous. She knew what her answer would be when he asked that question. She needed him and Bonnie, too. Her whole life seemed to have been lived just to share their lives and their love.